In That Other Dimension

Matty Millard

Enjoy!!

Published by Off The Shelf Publishing Ltd
Copyright © Matty Millard 2014
All rights reserved.
ISBN: 978-0-9926971-0-5

WITH SPECIAL
THANKS

To Jezza, Laura, Mike and Stacey for proof-reading my many attempts to write something half-decent, and to all my friends and family for their encouragement.

CHAPTER 1

It is a little known fact that every red telephone box in England contains a portal to a parallel dimension. This is activated by an amazing technology which our fantastic telecoms engineers have stumbled upon without ever actually realizing.

It is equally little known that this portal is activated simply by the phone number dialled in that box.

Had Carlos Ernesto Amadeus Von Schnaart had even an inkling of this then he may never have used the phone box in the first place. This presence of mind however was unlikely, as he was completely and utterly battered. In fact, his alcohol-induced state was the only reason he got into the phone box in the first place. If he had left the Ocean Bar in Soho, London, two tequilas earlier he would never have decided to call his on/off girlfriend Maria at 3:37 AM to slur declarations of undying love to her voicemail...again.

In a perverse way, his semi-conscious drunken stupor really helped him deal with the situation. Carlos assumed that the green smoke which slowly engulfed the telephone box on Soho Rd was just someone nearby smoking a huge spliff. He also assumed that the slow dimming of light towards total blackness was merely the act of his eyes closing over a prolonged period of time. And the feeling of travelling through 497 different parallel dimensions in three seconds to get to the destination which he had unwittingly dialled, was clearly just Carlos falling over.

It should be noted that in the field of dimensions, parallel means parallel only in that the dimensions exist at the same time as each other. In no other way are they parallel. For example, if you draw two parallel lines they never cross and carry on in the same direction. Parallel dimensions are by nature quite squiggly and their direction is definitely rndamo. (For the duration of this book the word random will be spelt randomly using the letters of the words random, for no other reason than I like it.)

Incidentally, had Carlos exited the phone box in these three seconds, he would have been stuck in a special place between parallel dimensions that doesn't really exist. Regardless of the fact that no one has ever returned from there, and it is not actually known whether anyone has even been there (as no-one has returned to tell us), rumour has it that the entire place is colourless and consists of no physical elements at all. This lack of physical elements means no gravitational force, so anyone stuck there would be floating around in nothingness with no control over where they are going. Not that there is anything to go and see anyway.

So, even though Carlos was thoroughly perplexed, a little bit irritated and unbelievably hung over when he finally woke up, he'd had quite a lucky escape really. Unfortunately that didn't make him feel any better, as nobody in his new surroundings could tell him that.

Carlos stumbled out of the phone box he had fallen asleep in the night before and rubbed his stinging eyes. He looked around in amazement, decided that he was still dreaming, went back into the phone box, and closed his eyes.

Two hours later he came round again. His headache was starting to subside so maybe today wouldn't be as bad as he feared, although he definitely wouldn't be drinking tequila again for a while.

He stretched - not very well because he was in a phone box - and decided to venture back out into the real world, hoping that no-one he knew would see him.

As he stepped out of the phone box, he had a strange feeling of déjà vu, and remembered the "dream" he'd had two hours earlier.

That's right, they were still there.

CHAPTER 2

Ducks.

Everywhere.

Nothing else in sight.

Stretching from his feet all the way to the horizon all Carlos could see was ducks. And these weren't just your regular kind of ducks. Well, they looked like your standard mallard, every single one of them – yellow beak, beady eyes, green head, flapping wings. The trouble was that they were approximately 80 feet tall and liked pecking.

Carlos checked his pockets for evidence of hallucinogenic substances but couldn't find any. His heart sank as he realized that they may not be a figment of his imagination after all. He climbed back in the telephone box to think about things for a little while.

Now is probably a good time to explain a little bit

about our man here, Carlos Ernesto Amadeus Von Schnaart. He was almost exactly the stereotype usually associated with an average Mexican male. Tall, olive skinned, black hair heavily gelled to one side. Smooth talking, definitely a ladies man. Likes a drink. Scottish.

Oh, and Carlos was extremely relaxed. So relaxed, in fact, that many of his friends back in his original dimension had feared that he might one day fall asleep and forget to wake up. So relaxed that a really, really, really scary man in a balaclava could balance an AK47 on his shoulder, fire a few rounds into a nearby building whilst chanting satanic rituals of death manically in a dead language, and he'd merely say "Hey bud, you wouldn't happen to have an ear-plug spare would you?"

So you'd imagine that he might be better equipped than your average human being to cope with his somewhat interesting situation.

Carlos sat in the corner[1], rocking from side to side, and for some reason the only thought he had in his head was that he really wished he had a huge loaf of bread.

---

1   Technically he was in all four corners. He was in a phone box.

CHAPTER 3

Carlos erupted from his state of shock with a cry, and an expression of hope and desperation etched across his face. He snatched the phone off its hook and punched in Maria's telephone number as fast as his fingers would allow him. He raised the phone to his ear... no dial tone.

"Damn it," he uttered under his breath as he scrabbled around in his pocket. He located a 20 pence piece, pushed it into the slot and redialled. Much to his surprise and relief it rang. And even more strangely, somebody answered.

"Maria! Maria!" Carlos cried, before the recipient had chance to speak. "Help me! I dunno what's... something really strange is happening to me!"

"Quack," was the solemn reply.

"I'm in a phone box! Please come and...." His voice tailed off quickly, as he realised it wasn't the jovial greeting Maria usually answered her phone with.

"Quack," repeated the voice on the other end.

Incidentally, dialling Maria's number had not been a

bad idea on Carlos's behalf. Unfortunately he had failed to enter a valid area code, country, galaxy, universe and dimension code, all of which are needed to successfully call somebody in another dimension. The previous night Carlos had been struggling with his short term memory. This had resulted in the input of Maria's phone number three times, plus the three extra "lucky" 7's needed to activate "Traveller Mode".

Carlos slumped once more to the floor when the phone box started to vibrate in time with a loud, rhythmic knocking on the roof. The metal split, revealing a huge, black, beady eye and a rather dangerous looking beak. It didn't look like the pecking had finished, so Carlos sprang to his feet and made a run for it.

As he sprinted through the maze of webbed feet and birds legs, it dawned upon him that the phone box currently being destroyed might represent his only chance of returning back home. Although Carlos felt a little dismayed at the thought of spending the rest of his life amongst 80 foot tall ducks, he decided he'd rather that than be pecked to death.

Carlos ran. He ran and ran and ran. And Carlos wasn't known for his running. In fact the only previous time he had ever run as fast as this was one morning when he had almost arrived at work for a mundane day of number-crunching before realising that he'd left the iron on. As we already know, Carlos is not usually a worrier. But this time he'd left the iron attached to two welded together saucepans, inside which he was simulating the splitting of the atom using some cheddar and a miniature colander. Carlos wasn't so much a scientist, as that would imply he knew what he was doing, but he did have a keen and exploratory interest in physics. That time, he'd run for ten whole minutes and just prevented a minor explosion.

By now, he'd been running for twenty minutes and quite frankly he wasn't enjoying it anymore. He could still see nothing but webbed feet and huge knobbly knees and he was getting rather fed up of it.

Carlos took a glance over his shoulder and could no longer see the phone box he had arrived in, but more importantly, the ducks around him didn't seem to be trying to destroy anything. He must have run far enough from those who had been disturbed by his arrival. Relieved, he looked forward again just in time to see the cliff edge he was about to run off.

Unfortunately he couldn't stop in time.

The severity of the situation hit Carlos immediately. This wasn't your average cliff, it was the kind of cliff you might expect if you are in a dimension where the sole inhabitants are 80 foot tall ducks. So as Carlos the part-time physicist plummeted towards the ground four miles below him he started to wonder not whether he would survive, but how far underground his momentum would take him. The ground eventually came into focus, and when it was around 20 metres away Carlos closed his eyes and waited for impact.

Meanwhile, back in Carlos's home dimension the mysterious disappearance of the phone box was creating a few newspaper headlines. Of course, it began as a very minor headline in the local gazette, but after numerous similar incidents it seemed that phone box theft was a new craze amongst the youth culture in

England. However, this was small fry compared to some of the other strange goings on which had happened since his departure. Various theories were flying around to explain them; Undetected life-forms caused by genetic mutation during the Chernobyl disaster; the new "Ten Plagues" caused by an argument between the second coming of Christ and an Egyptian oil baron; some unbelievably bad attempts at cloning; and even video games come to life were just some of the rumours. Whatever the cause, there were now some very strange creatures roaming the Earth.

CHAPTER 4

Terrence Smith woke up in a daze. He didn't quite know what to make of the events of the previous three seconds, but he sure as hell hadn't enjoyed them. It had felt exactly like what he thought doing a bungee would be like, except it was less fun and only lasted three seconds. And he was in a phone box. Terrence didn't know you could do bungee jumps **inside** phone boxes. He was very confused.

Now Terrence feeling confused wasn't a particularly new concept. In fact it was something he had lived with for most of his life. People had regularly told him he wasn't the sharpest tool in the box and this baffled him even more. It meant that most of his life was spent with a headache whilst contemplating the similarities between himself and an electric drill[2].

---

2   Drills are smarter. In the toolbox intelligence hierarchy, Terrence is just below "clamp" and directly above "sledgehammer".

This time, I'm sure you'll agree, Terrence could be forgiven for being confused. He had been standing in a phone box, minding his own business and enjoying his simple yet pleasing life. He liked the different sounds you get from pressing the different numbered keys, and on finding twenty pence on the pavement, had been performing his self-composed phone-box ditty. He'd just worked out a new solo which he was really rocking out on, when suddenly the world started to spin around very quickly.

And that's pretty much where things stood with Terrence at this moment in time. Oh, and his sister had passed out and he didn't like the green sky and blue floor he could see through the glass, or the evil birds which flew below him with their feet sticking up in the air. Terrence was so terrified that he couldn't even remember how to open the phone box door[3]. It was probably a good thing that he hadn't worked out that he was standing on his head in an upside down phone box. Even one more minuscule iota of confusion would probably have blown his tiny little mind.

---

3   Push…

CHAPTER 5

Carlos hit the ground with an almighty bump. He lay very still, expecting it all to end at any moment. Thoughts and memories from throughout his life started to flood his mind. He didn't fight them, he lay back and let them flow. After all that's what you're supposed to do in these situations isn't it? You know, just to pass the time while you're waiting.

So what happens now? thought Carlos. He didn't know what to expect. Nothing? The Grim Reaper to appear on horseback with his scythe? Would an evil black stork swoop down to take him away?

Carlos and gullible were not two words you would usually put in the same sentence, but Carlos's mothers' hatred of the father he had never met, meant that Carlos did believe that as a baby he had been hidden behind the family gooseberry bush by a graceful white stork. Picturing his mother telling him that story every birthday since he was born, he began to wonder whether he'd ever see his family and friends again.

After what must have been the most stressful half

an hour of Carlos's life, he was still waiting for something to happen. As it hadn't, he decided to open his eyes, stand up, brush himself off and see what Heaven looked like.

Oh no! thought Carlos. *It can't be. What have I done to deserve this?*

Now any human being in Carlos's situation would have looked around him and assumed he was in Hell. So Carlos was being completely rational in this presumption, but what he didn't know was that he was actually on an alternate Earth in a parallel dimension made entirely of candy-floss. When the sun rose, the rain stopped and the dark red surroundings became the more friendly and fluffy pink usually associated with candy-floss, this would become more obvious.

* * *

Now would probably be a good time to give a brief history of inter-dimensional travel and explain how Carlos miraculously avoided plunging to an untimely death.

Although this book previously credited our dimension's telecommunications industry[4] with the unwitting invention of inter-dimensional travel, they

---

4   It's our dimension's telecommunications industry based on the assumption that this book has not been translated into some bizarre and unknown language such as... English... and sent through some kind of field-time vortex into a parallel dimension where you, but not I, live. Although, thinking about it, I'll probably be there somewhere, in some form, maybe even reading this book. I bet I don't like it and I find at least three spelling mistakes.

were technically beaten to it by approximately eight million years, by our near-neighbours from the second dimension once removed. This dimension was commonly known as Utopia, and the Utopians actually meant to invent it. Their initial testing had quickly established that one couldn't easily "go on holiday" to another dimension and then come back, as you needed to know the correct number to enter into your dimensional control pad for the return journey. Although nobody had ever got this right and returned, it was still obvious to those who hadn't travelled that something tangible had happened and the people hadn't just disappeared. In the first experiment the traveller was replaced with a miniature carpet gibbon. The reason for this is as follows:

To stop the outer-dimensional universe from getting too heavy on one side, there needs to be some kind of inter-dimensional balancing. So every time a person crosses dimensions they swap places with another being, selected completely at orndma from the one they arrive in.

The fact that nobody had ever returned to Utopia meant that people were not so keen to travel to new dimensions, however the technology was identified as an excellent way to rid your planet of all things untrustworthy, evil and just downright pesky. So for years the technology was used for deportation. And although the nature of inter-dimensional balancing's replacement selection was entirely mndaro you usually got something nicer and more interesting in return.

After a while, Utopia was rid of all things criminal and everything was hunky dory. However, as you probably know, people are never happy and all of a sudden "The Powers That Be" decided that they wanted rid of those who weren't pulling their weight. So anyone seen to be slovenly, unclean or in any way removed from society were under threat.

One fateful morning, now known as "D"-day[5], two harmless beggars from the primitive region known as Ug were selected for banishment. With the exception of an angry badger squirrel who caused a minor commotion when he buried the Head Customs Officer's nuts, recent trade-offs from these exchanges had been quite pleasant so security was a little lax.

Unfortunately the receipt of an Allosaurus and a Tyrannosaurus Rex into the arrivals lounge resulted in the consumption of the entire population of Utopia, severely hindering further testing of cross-dimensional travel.

The inhabitants of London had also had similar troubles with the 80 foot mallard which replaced Carlos. However the duck rampaged South through Europe and finally found a warm spot in the Mediterranean to roost.

On a brighter note, in their new dimension the two beggars from Ug found a new vocation in life; clubbing dinosaurs and starting the human race.

And eight million years later, the inventor and first ever inter-dimensional traveller from Utopia had grown bored of living in a dimension made of candy floss and decided to move on to pastures new. Unfortunately for him, not only did he drop his satchel

---

5   D for Dino, contrary to popular belief

containing many years of research and all his back-up instruments, but he managed to dmaron-ly exchange places with Carlos approximately 1.5 seconds before the expected collision with the ground. He was probably lucky that he had very little time to assess his situation before he came crashing down at a high speed into his new, very temporary, surroundings.

CHAPTER 6

There was a stirring on the phone box roof[6].

"Hey!" said Terrence, "You're back!"

"Just about," replied Maria groggily. "What happened?"

"I don't know. Everything was all normal and then the world began to spin and then you fell on the floor and then the phone box flew up into the air..." Terrence gasped for breath before continuing at some pace. "And then we landed and now the world is upside down and I don't like it. Look, the birds fly with their feet in the air!

By the end of the sentence Terrence was almost shrieking. His sister Maria was well used to this, he always panicked when confused.

"Oh Terrence, don't be silly," she fussed. "You should start by standing on your feet, you silly banana, then you'll see that the birds aren't upside-down."

Terrence felt rather foolish as he turned himself

---

6   Floor

around the right way but began to feel better as six pints of blood flowed from his head back towards his feet. It only took a few minutes for his complexion to fade from a deep puce and Terrence was back to his normal dopey, but non-hysterical, self.

"There, that's better isn't it?" said Maria.

Terrence nodded, feeling much better. He followed Maria's lead and hauled himself to his feet, ready to explore their new surroundings. Maria led the way across the rocky and uneven terrain in her usual confident manner, chattering away to Terrence as she did so.

"Oh, look over there Terrence, it's delightful isn't it? All the sand, and the open spaces. There's no-one here, it's so peaceful!"

It didn't matter that Terrence muttered in agreement, Maria hadn't stopped talking for about twenty minutes.

"I can see a little spot of sunlight in that far corner. We should walk over there and then have a nice rest. You could do with a sit down, we should be taking it easy after your little episode. Do you want to sit down now?"

"No Maria, for the thousandth time, I'm fine!" he snapped, exasperated at her constant questions. It's not like she paused to listen to his answers anyway.

"Okay!" she huffed. "I'm just checking! I always have to, you know? You remember that one time you rang me from the park to tell me you'd had an accident on the slide don't you?"

"That was ages ago!" Terrence whined, the conversation not improving his mood.

"Still, the principle's the same. If you'd had told me

at the time that the slide was stuck around your bottom you'd never have got yourself wedged on that bus would you?"

"Well, no… but I didn't want you to worry did I?"

"It was even more worrying when that hobo jumped on the slide from the top level of the bus though wasn't it? I swear… if you hadn't got on the bus wedged in a slide I'd have thought it was that bang on the head that made you do so many silly things."

Terrence didn't reply, he knew there was no point arguing. She always did this. Terrence knew he had done lots of stupid things in the past but she wasn't always right. Granted, she was far more intelligent than he was, but Maria never acknowledged the times he had been helpful. He'd punched out countless idiot boyfriends for her, and every time she had incorrectly thought she could have handled it better herself.

As they trekked across the dusty plains in search of life, water or somewhere that looked vaguely hospitable, the argumentative siblings continued doing what they did best. Maria constantly checked on Terrence after his little panicky episode, whilst Terrence worried about not knowing where they were, or who else might be around. He was decidedly sheepish, his watch flitting all over the place, constantly expecting the unexpected.

There was a fundamental flaw in Terrence's thinking here. If you expect the unexpected and the unexpected happens, then technically you were expecting it so you should be able to cope. In addition if you are expecting the unexpected then for it to truly be unexpected then it must be even more unexpected than what you might expect unexpected to be. So by expecting the unexpected the truly unexpected is going to cause a lot more trouble. But if you don't expect anything, then it'll probably just be a pleasant surprise.

Anyway, the unexpected didn't arrive but Maria and Terrence were starting to get thirsty. Maria had seen places like this on TV before, and although it wasn't particularly hot she knew that food and water would be scarce. Aiming towards some rocky mountains in the distance, she hoped this might provide a change in geology and somewhere they might find a waterfall or a natural spring.

Approaching the cliffs she spied what might be a path between the rocks.

A mountain pass would be perfect, she thought as she led Terrence into the opening where the path began. After about 200 yards, the open rocky expanse started to narrow as the land became more jagged and harsh on either side. As they walked further, they found themselves following a small winding path between two gigantic cliffs, so steep that the tops were not even in sight. As they followed it deeper into the canyon, the light began to dim and they wished they'd stayed put until morning.

However it was pointless turning back now, they'd never get back to the phone box before nightfall and they didn't want to get lost in the dark. So they continued along the pathway, hoping to find somewhere to shelter until morning. Little did they know that it wasn't actually night-time, they were merely burrowing deeper and deeper underground into the darkness.

* * *

Maria awoke first and it took her a while to recognise the little hollow they had settled in for a rest. She slowly sat upright and pushed her brunette curls away from her face. She was quite a pretty girl (when it wasn't dark) and had deep brown eyes with long, thick eyelashes, perfect for her favourite pastime of flirting.

This morning Maria was a little puzzled. It felt like she'd been asleep for hours but it was still pitch black. She'd never been anywhere with such long night times before. After a while, her eyes adjusted and she could make out a faint silhouette which resembled a terrace of houses in a clearing at the end of the passage. Well, not quite houses, but it looked as if there were windows and doors carved into the rock face. It was almost like a cave-man version of a typical terraced road back in London. She crept away from the nook in which they had settled, careful not to wake Terrence. As she got nearer to the houses she was sure she could hear laughing.

There must be people! Maria thought. Buoyed by excitement she stepped up her pace and headed for the noises.

Maria rushed across the clearing she had arrived in, and in her eagerness tripped over a jagged edge, falling with some force on her shoulder. Through the throbbing pain she could have sworn she heard a gasp. All of a sudden her confidence and excitement dissipated into apprehension and fear. She didn't know what was there, and although she couldn't see anything she had a nagging feeling that she was being watched.

Taking a couple of minutes to recover, she regained

her composure and looked around. On the reddish tinged rocks she could see darting shadows. They were everywhere, dancing around her, in and out of the nooks and crannies.

Don't panic, she told herself. *It's just your eyes playing tricks.*

But still the shadows played. It didn't matter how many times she tried to reassure herself that it was just the darkness making her imagine things, she didn't quite believe it. She lay still, trying to blank out the noises and ignore the shadows. Maria had always had an active imagination, and waking up frozen stiff with paranoia after a bad dream was a fairly regular occurrence.

She lay, gazing around nervously. The shadows still hadn't stopped darting, but it had been a while since she tripped and nothing had happened so Maria began to relax a little. Even so, she rose to her feet, intent on returning to wake Terrence before continuing her exploration.

As she stood, she felt rapid movements all around her and heard the patter of scurrying feet. The silence was deafening as she tried to scream Terrence's name. It felt like the entire world piled in on top of her in an instant and dragged her away into the dark unknown.

CHAPTER 7

"Come on Mr Fluffy Rabbit, you can do it!" shouted Terrence as Mr Fluffy Rabbit revved himself up for the pole vault in the inaugural Champion of the Wooden Hutch Competition. He bobbed forwards and back, forwards and back before launching himself into the sprint run-up. Terrence turned over and dribbled a little, but didn't quite wake.

Mr Fluffy Rabbit threw his pole in front of him and sailed gracefully into the air, smiling and waving to the cameras. The fans cheered and sang his name "Fluffy! Fluffy! Fluffy!" as Mr Fluffy Rabbit cleared the bar and landed with a splattering squelch into a rotating meat grinder.

Terrence sat up as quick as a shot, the sweat pouring from his forehead. He looked around for rabbits. There were none. And no entrails either.

Phew.

There was also no Maria, but Terrence naturally assumed she had needed a wee so had gone to the bathroom.

He turned over and was just dropping back to sleep as an ice-cold draft swept over him and the world accelerated away at warp speed. His eardrums screeched with pain.

Terrence smiled. It was just like his favourite roller-coaster in Blackpool.

A couple of minutes later Terrence had completed a loop the loop, numerous high speed twists and had been climbing steadily upwards for a while. He bravely opened his eyes to see how high he was. Strangely enough there were no rails, fellow passengers or roller-coasters anywhere in sight. All Terrence could see was the colour white. He wasn't bound, as far as he could tell, but somehow he couldn't even move a finger. It was as if he was held captive in a pure white cell moulded perfectly to his body. The piercing screams continued, tormenting his eardrums.

This was quite a lot for Terrence to take in and his heart and mind raced through all sorts of possibilities. He pushed against his invisible restraints with all of his might but he couldn't make any headway. As he pressed and wiggled and slithered, his cell became tighter. He felt his breathing race and his thoughts collide. Terrence began to panic, he was convinced that he would live out the rest of his life in this incomprehensible state.

After trying to move every part of his body to no avail, Terrence was exhausted and stood defeated. He slumped, upright, in his body tight cocoon, head banging from the constant screaming. After a few minutes of stillness, resignation and feeling sorry for himself, he began to regain some composure and started to breathe naturally again.

Terrence's thoughts turned to his sister Maria and he wondered where she was. Although he really hoped she was safe, he secretly wished she was here with him, to think of a plan like she always did. *She always gets me out of trouble,* he thought as he tried to imagine what Maria would do in his situation.

Although she came across as quite scatter-brained, Terrence knew that she was methodical when under pressure. The first thing she would do, would be to work out she could do, and what she couldn't. Well that was easy really. Terrence could breathe, and that was about it.

Terrence surprised himself by following up an observation with a trail of thought.

I can breathe, that means there must be air! Terrence's brain had slipped into reverse and was ready to leave the garage.

*And I've been here a while, so there must be a lot of it! Unless…*Terrence had remembered to open the garage door and had reached the driveway.

There must be a hole 'cos I ain't dead yet! Eureka. Terrence had slammed the clutch into the floor and first gear was engaged.

Re-invigorated by his belief that there must be some way out of his predicament, he searched high and low trying to find a hole in the wall of his cell. He wiggled all of his fingers and toes vigorously. He stretched up high and tried to detect a space using his over developed left nipple. Finally he stuck out his tongue and tried to find a crevice to lick his way out through. Amazingly, he found a slight chink and licked and licked like nothing you've ever seen before. The thought of orange ice lollies filled his mind and

Terrence was happy once again.

* * *

The world was a swimming darkness in front of Maria's eyes. It *glibbed* and *globbed* and *glawed* as her senses slowly returned. Recent memories flashed through her mind, one at a time. She remembered waking up in a phone box, laughing at Terrence and then hiking across a desert. Falling asleep in a dark cave, waking to strange sounds and mysterious shadows. Being dragged along the floor by unknown captors. Maria froze as she remembered that she was probably in grave danger.

Her eyes eventually started to find focus and Maria tried to assess where she was and what was happening. She was sat bolt upright in a giant wooden chair, the back of which towered high above her. Thick ropes cut into her wrists and ankles, restraining her from any sort of movement. Her gigantic chair was dwarfed by the cave it was in, the walls of which she could just make out thanks to the slowly blinking blue light on the ceiling. With every flash she could see just a little bit more.

Around her she could see nothing but shadows, darting aggressively like those she had seen outside. With every blue flash of the light, hundreds of silhouetted creatures pointed and screamed silently at her, only to vanish and re-appear seconds later. The shadows seemed to be alive.

How can I have been captured by shadows? thought Maria, frightened by the strange world she had found herself in.

"TERRENCE!" she screamed, but no sound left her mouth.

Panicked, she fought against her bonds but they wouldn't budge an inch.

Maria had never been completely trapped before and she didn't like it. She was so upset that she couldn't even bring herself to tell the shadows that it was rude to point.

She sat as calmly as she could manage, and waited for Terrence to come and find her. She desperately hoped that the shadows wouldn't find him first.

Two hours later Maria was still stumped and Terrence hadn't come to rescue her yet. She had thought through pretty much every option she had, but could think of absolutely no way out of her current predicament. She was bound so tightly that unless someone miraculously came to untie her she would be stuck there forever. Maria resorted to Plan B - hoping it would all just go away.

She relaxed and tried to forget about the situation, instead focusing on the life she had left behind her in London.

Maria's life had always been interesting, despite her desire for an easy one. She was trusting and good-natured, too trusting many people told her.

It's probably this that gets me into so much trouble she thought. *I've lost jobs because of my friends and been cheated on numerous times by that scumbag Carlos. Even this whole situation seems to have been caused by Terrence messing around in a phone box.*

Despite all this, Maria smiled at the thought of her friends and family.

I miss them all, especially Carlos.

Carlos was the love of her life but he had always treated her awfully. He had a drinking problem which generally resulted in him cheating on Maria, or calling her up to confess and apologise about something, or someone, he had done. On the night before her fateful phone box journey with Terrence he had obviously been on another bender. He'd gone out for "a quiet one with the lads" and hadn't returned home. It was becoming a trend and they argued repeatedly about this.

Carlos did have a completely different side to him though. Maria remembered a time when her father had broken his leg in a horse riding accident. Carlos had travelled two hundred miles to Manchester just to do a supermarket shop for him. It was that kind of generosity which meant that Carlos managed to charm his way into forgiveness every time, sometimes despite her better judgment. Maria lay back and let her thoughts fill up with good memories.

CHAPTER 8

Carlos awoke sitting on a carved wooden chair in a crystal clean white laboratory. About five feet away from him sat Maria, who had a strange metal bowl sitting upside-down on her head. She was littered with intra-veinous tubes and was attached to a complicated looking machine by a long black wire. On the other side of Maria sat Terrence who appeared to be trying to lick her.

"Strange," thought Carlos. Although on reflection, this was Terrence.

Carlos took the metal bowl off his head and pulled the tubing out of his wrist.

"Maria!" he whispered.

Her eyes were glazed over and she was completely oblivious to his presence.

"Maria!" He shook her gently. Still nothing.

Looking behind her he could see a huge screen, on which there was a picture of London Bridge. It flickered and was replaced by a picture of Carlos himself!

Looking good, but put some clothes on! he urged himself, glad that no-one else was awake to see the image.

On the screen behind Terrence were images of refreshing looking orange ice lollies. Carlos could see a wire connecting the screen to Terrence's helmet.

It must be something to do with their thoughts, Carlos reasoned. Looking back at Terrence's, that would at least explain the licking.

Carlos began to grin when he realised that Maria must be thinking of him in the nuddy, but any of *those* thoughts quickly disappeared when he heard footsteps approaching. Carlos ran across the room and hid behind a pillar.

Striding into the laboratory was a tall and clean cut man in a pristine white lab coat, which hung over his shiny knee length boots.

"Impossible!" the scientist cried. "He's escaped!"

Waving his arms around in a frenzy, he thumped his monocle back to his eye and pounded away on a nearby computer keyboard.

Eventually he found the screen he wanted and he peered at a long list of numbers. Springing to his feet, he shouted out at the top of his voice.

"He's not been gone long! Close the doors!"

The instructions were aimed towards the three strange looking creatures that had followed him in. One appeared to be a human torso on a rickety looking tripod, one looked like a cereal box on wonky trolley wheels and the other resembled a pigeon with a horse's head. Each of them went off slowly in different directions, two of them squeaking and creaking, and the third crashing to the ground every time its body weight outbalanced its wings.

Carlos didn't know what to do. Should he get out of the lab, make a plan and then try to get back in later to rescue Maria and Terrence? Or should he try to stay hidden somewhere inside? The first *swoosh* and *bump* of a door closing made him one hundred percent sure that he had to run. Sneaking back in with a plan to rescue Maria and Terrence would be far better than hiding until this crazy scientist guy, who was probably armed, searched every inch of his lair and found him.

Carlos ran. He ran and ran and ran. He ran straight across the laboratory, pushing aside the scientist as he went. The man sprawled across the stone floor, shouting for help. Seizing the couple of seconds he had, Carlos opportunistically grabbed a couple of items off the lab bench. Struggling to run at the same time, he wedged a torch and a book into his satchel.

A satchel? he thought. *I don't even own a satchel! Where on earth has that come from?* Deciding that he had better things to worry about, he embraced his new man-bag and looked ahead.

Carlos ran in the same direction that the cereal box on trolley wheels had set off, having assumed that the creature's steering abilities wouldn't be the best. Sure enough, Carlos easily overtook the stricken guard who was wedged against a wall half-way along the corridor. He relaxed a little as he spied daylight and gained fresh impetus as he smelled the fresh air. Once outside, Carlos watched the entrance to the lair whilst he caught his breath. He only dared to stay there a few seconds though, he needed to get away quickly.

Carlos was puzzled. The land outside the scientist's lair was so vast and empty. He scanned the horizon for something, a landmark, somewhere to shelter.

That'll do nicely! Carlos thought as he spied a familiar looking silhouette on the horizon.

His spirits were instantly lifted by the sight of the phone-box. Yes, it did appear that he was stranded in a strange land where his girlfriend and her brother were being held captive by an evil scientist, but at least he could call someone and get some help. There was bound to be a phone directory in there.

Carlos felt more and more confident as he got closer to the phone box, the one thing familiar to him in this strange place.

Unfortunately, when he reached the phone box he had a welcoming committee.

CHAPTER 9

In a dimension not too far away, a teenage boy was roaming around with two giant pimples on his chin which would completely change the lives of our intrepid travellers.

These pimples were absolutely massive. They were both so ram-jam-full of custard it was unbelievable, and were so close together that they were destined to join and form one massive pimple at some time. That time was fast approaching.

The most interesting thing about these particular pimples is that they were both actually separate dimensions in their own right. Imagine that, two whole dimensions on a greasy teenager's chin about to merge into each other. Basically, our teenager here is happily walking around in his own dimension[7], with two parallel and slowly merging dimensions on his chin, completely oblivious that the events about to happen on his face will actually change the entire course of

---

7   I told you dimensions were squiggly

history. The squiggliness of the dimensional structure was the reason why Carlos was walking around in two different dimensions at the same time.

Unfortunately for Carlos, when it happens, the inevitable merging of a dimension made of candy-floss with a dimension where a crazy scientist lives means that anyone who happens to exist inside both of these dimensions will be forced to relinquish one of its existences. We can't have things existing twice in one dimension, that would just be silly.

CHAPTER 10

Carlos was disappointed at having arrived in Hell, but didn't waste time feeling sorry for himself. He was on his feet and ready to explore. Whilst surveying the scene, he noticed a satchel lying on the ground nearby.

A brief flick through the bag revealed a pile of complicated scientific drawings, a folder and some sophisticated looking electrical equipment. The physicist in Carlos was automatically intrigued. Even though he had no idea what it did, he desperately wanted to play with the new toy he had found. However, based on his recent duck experience, Carlos was wary of what this new world may contain and wanted to make sure he was safe before doing anything else. He put the contraption away, slung the satchel over his shoulder and went for a stroll.

It quickly struck Carlos that his new surroundings were very different to his preconceived idea of Hell. In the books he had read, Hell was usually portrayed as a dark underground world with fires burning in the skies, towering jagged cliffs and huge cavernous pits full of bones and skulls. Carlos was walking along a meandering meadow path, well more bouncing along, except that the rain was causing his feet to stick to the candy floss floor a little.

Skinny tree trunks with huge round colourful flat tops stood proudly by the side of the road. In Hell you might expect a vulture to be surveying the scene from a gnarled dead branch. Sugary streams fizzed gently by. Carlos had feared raging lava waterfalls.

But the most obvious difference between this place and Carlos's preconception of Hell was that it appeared to be getting lighter, and he swore he could hear birds singing. Everyone knows that Hell is always dark and has huge speakers blaring out speed metal all day long.[8]

When the sickly yellow sun started to peek over the pink fluffy hills on the horizon, Carlos finally convinced himself that maybe he wasn't actually dead, and that he hadn't ended up in Hell. Carlos didn't even bother to wonder why not, as he knew it would be very confusing. He just laid back and enjoyed the sunrise.

As the sun rose higher in the sky it revealed rolling pink meadows with yellow buttercups stretching out to the hills in the distance. Carlos had settled down next to a tinkling brook which met a long river, flowing gently through a picturesque valley. At the far end of the river he could see a waterfall gushing through a high gorge of pink rock. Nearby, a small rounded bridge over the brook looked like it might be made of dark chocolate. Round, flat lollipop trees and huge candy canes were dotted around in fields lined by bushy marshmallow hedges. The most intriguing features of this new land

---

8   It sounds good. I'd quite like to visit.

however, were the quaint gingerbread houses in the distance, from which a number of early rising jelly babies had appeared.

Now the possibility of there being some sort of non-gigantic-duck related civilization in this land was enough to lift Carlos's spirits, especially as everything looked so nice and friendly. The rain had long stopped, and where the deep red puddles had been the candy floss floor was drying out into a springy pink carpet. Seeing this, Carlos felt incredibly hungry. He hadn't eaten for hours, and faced with scenes from his childhood fantasies, Carlos set about fulfilling his hunger with relish.

An hour later, Carlos felt quite sick. It reminded him of the feeling he used to get at around 11 o' clock on Easter morning, when despite his Mom's warnings not to eat all his chocolate at once he had devoured four Easter eggs in a row and was suffering from severe tummy-ache and a major sugar rush. He lay down for a while and didn't notice that the jelly babies he had seen earlier were approaching in vast numbers.

A gentle coughing awoke Carlos from his slumber. He sat up with a groan and looked around dazedly. There was a crowd of multi-coloured jelly babies standing in a large ring around him[9]. Now nine times out of ten Carlos would have assumed that this would be quite a pleasurable situation but unfortunately these jelly babies all seemed a little angry and were waving some rather sharp looking pitchforks at him.

"Hello?" he said quietly.

One of the jelly babies stepped forward and

---

9   I say large. The ring was large but the jelly babies weren't. They were, as usual, about 2 cm high.

proceeded to bellow at Carlos in quite an aggressive manner.

"Argghawwawarramanna[10]!!" he bawled whilst waving his pitchfork violently and pointing at Carlos.

"Er... sorry?" Carlos responded politely. "Do you speak English?"

"Ha[11]! Larrikarnafeeeesh[12]!!" was the reply.

"Larrikarnafeeeesh!!!" repeated the others at the tops of their annoyingly squeaky little voices.

"I guess not," said Carlos, rolling his eyes. Interpreting his bafflement as disrespect, the jelly babies lowered their pitch forks, waved animatedly and charged towards him.

Carlos calmly stood as the jelly babies repeatedly stabbed the leather of his brown suede shoes, oblivious to the fact that it wasn't ever going to hurt him. After a while he began to chuckle. *They don't give up easily* he thought to himself. It wasn't long though, before his amusement turned to irritation. Their constant screeching voices were beginning to grate on him, so he located the leader and put him in his pocket.

Eating the leader did cross his mind, but Carlos was still feeling pretty sick from his sugary gluttony earlier. He picked up a few more of the other pitchfork waving residents though, so he would have a nice little snack for later on.

In the distance Carlos could see that one or two of the more sensible jelly babies had scarpered back to the safety of their gingerbread houses. As he had nothing

---

10   Jelly-speak for "You ate our bridge so you must die! You meanie."

11   "Ha!"

12   "Poke him!"

better to do, Carlos followed them. He wanted to explore the populated part of his new surroundings.

CHAPTER 11

Carlos was gnawing away enthusiastically on a gingerbread chimney when the cake dragon approached.

"That's not really very nice is it?" asked the cake dragon in a silky smooth voice, a large drool of cream running down her neck. "There's jelly babies live in that house you know."

Carlos turned around and looked up.

"Ah," he said. "You're quite big."

Contrary to everything else in the tiny land of confectionary, the dragon was huge. She was made of cake upon cake upon cake upon cake. Just one of her legs must have contained more than a hundred black forest gateaux on top of each other.

Carlos looked up at her in a fearful but amused admiration. He'd never seen anything like it! The dragon was made of all kinds of cake. Fruit cake, chocolate cake, apple pie, Swiss roll – everything you could think of stitched seamlessly together into one. She was a ginormous patchwork patisserie.

"Yes I am quite big," replied the dragon kindly.

"And I'm only seven years old so I have lots of growing still to do. When I'm older I'll be as big as those mountains over there."

The dragon pointed out into the distance where Carlos could see two imposing mounds at the front of a large mountain range.

"That's my Mom on the left, and my Dad on the right. I usually sleep in the middle of them."

Carlos could see an empty little U shaped valley between the two mountains, which he guessed must be the space that the dragon had vacated.

"Anyway," said the baby cake dragon, trying to put on a menacing face by scrunching her chocolate éclair eyebrows together. "Why are you eating the houses? The jelly babies have never done anything to you."

"Erm.." mumbled Carlos, his mind desperately searching for an excuse before reverting to the composed manner which was more typical of him. "I was quite hungry I suppose, I hadn't eaten for two whole days before I got to this land and the sight of all of this food was just too much! What is this place called?" he asked.

"It's called Pink River," answered the cake dragon, still looking unimpressed.

"Oh right, Pink River. Nice name." He smiled, hoping that his natural charm might cut him some slack. "I come from a place very different to here, and this world is amazing! It's made of all the food I liked to eat when I was little. Do you not eat gingerbread then?"

"No!" said the dragon, astonished and pulling a disgusted face. "We eat candy floss of course, as it grows everywhere, and we eat some of the sweets you find on the trees. But mainly we eat the little rock creatures you see wandering around the fields. The jelly babies farm these and sell them at market every week."

"Oh right. Maybe this place isn't too different from where I live then," said Carlos, seeing the harvesting similarities between what Éclair ate and what he ate back at home. He stared up at the cake dragon, again unaware that there was a large gathering of jelly babies forming nearby.

All of a sudden they started to shout in their shrill little voices, their language still unfathomable to Carlos.

Carlos could see from the way that the jelly babies were pointing and waving that the conversation wasn't going to be very good for him. The cake dragon's éclair eyebrows were going into overdrive, and a look of bewilderment, disgust and then anger swept across her face.

"Is this true?" the dragon demanded of Carlos. "Have you kidnapped the jelly babies? They are my friends!" She finished her sentence with a wail of grief.

"Erm. Well.... No?" Carlos said. Lying was far harder when sober and this untruth didn't stick with the cake dragon. A minutes silence and a stern stare prompted an admission.

"I had to! They were attacking me!"

The dragon sighed, clearly unimpressed by Carlos's excuse. Quite how a six foot tall man couldn't defend himself against a few tiny jelly babies she did not know.

Through the quiet, Carlos could hear a shrill yelling coming from his top pocket, where he'd stored the jelly babies for later. He cringed as the cake dragon stared at him open mouthed.

Carlos reached inside his pocket and pulled the struggling jelly babies out. Unable to take his eyes off the cake dragon, he placed them on the floor and they rushed off back into the village, slamming their tiny gingerbread doors behind them.

"Why were you keeping them captive?" the cake dragon implored.

Carlos looked around, trying to think of something to say when the truth twigged in the cake dragon's mind.

"Were you....?" She paused and stared at Carlos, the guilt evident on his face. "Were you going to **eat** them?"

Carlos didn't have enough time to reply, the stuttering was enough of an admission for the cake dragon. Up to now Carlos had thought her quite sweet. Huge and intimidating yes, but sweet, and not only in the *"I'd like to eat you"* sense of the word. With a deafening roar, she breathed a powerful jet of squirty cream at Carlos, which threw him backwards onto the ground. The dragon stepped forward, placing a heavy sponge paw onto his chest, pinning him down.

"My friend," stated the cake dragon firmly, "I think it is time you met my parents."

CHAPTER 12

In a nearby dimension (which I would call X but it's already taken, so instead we'll refer to it as $E=mc^2$) Carlos's second existence was also struggling to make friends.

He looked grudgingly at the creatures guarding Terrence and Maria's phone box. In keeping with the oddities which Carlos had seen inside the mad scientist's lair, the guards appeared to be a strange concoction of species and implements.

One of the creatures had stepped out boldly before him. "And where do you think you're going?" asked the guard.

"I might tell you if you can tell me what the Hell you are supposed to be," snapped Carlos. Contrary to his usual relaxed nature, Carlos was a little bit irritated, but then he had just escaped from a mind-controlling maniac's lair where his girlfriend and her brother were still being held hostage.

His retort, laced with venom, caught the guard off-guard, a decidedly embarrassing thing to happen if you are a guard. To be fair though, the guard was a tortoise with a watermelon for a head so catching him unaware probably wasn't a one-off. A bright pink hyena with springs on his feet took over the role of spokesman from the dejected tortoise with relish.

"I.. I.. I'm a hyena with springs on my feet!!" he shrieked as he bounced over their heads, giggling hysterically. "And.. and he's a tortoise with a watermelon head!!! Whee he heee!!! And she's a galah with no wings!!! Ha ha ha!!" He breathed quickly before continuing in the same enthusiastic and hyperactive manner.

"What use is a flaming galah with no wings?" the hyena asked rhetorically as he flew marginally over Carlos's head. "Bout as useful as a chocolate teapot!! Ha ha ha!!! Or a cat-flap in a submarine!! Wheeeeeeee!"

The hyena was rewarded with a vicious peck when he settled next to the galah. She was not amused, and muttered something about waiting for a part so that she could have her new wheels fitted. The hyena went quiet and tears welled in his big bright eyes. The tortoise-melon had by this point regained his composure and continued the conversation slowly and methodically.

"You may notice that we are guarding your device of travel at the moment."

Device of travel? Carlos was smart enough to take in this information, but not let on that as far as he knew this was just a regular phone box.

"I have noticed, and it would be wonderful if you would step out of my way."

"I'm afraid that this is not possible," continued the tortoise-melon in his dreary low tone. "We are under strict instructions from our lord and creator to guard it so that he can learn from its special powers. He is the cleverest, and soon to be most powerful man in the universe. He made us as we are today and we have sworn to obey him at all times."

Carlos eyed the three strangely adapted creatures and dared to ask what could be a close to the bone question. What had he to lose? "So, erm…. Are you pleased with what he made you into?"

The tortoise-melon thought carefully before answering. "Yes I am. Initially I had my doubts I have to admit, as I found it rather difficult to see. At first the whole world was rather pink, but eventually I got used to it. Nowadays I just get the occasional seed in front of my eyes, but they can easily be blinked away." He sighed and continued. "It's been a really good head, and I never, ever, have a nasty taste in my mouth any more. I used to hate getting a dry throat in the summer, it really got me down."

"Are you serious?" asked Carlos. "You wear a watermelon on your head because you have a dry throat? Couldn't you just suck a mint or something?"

"No," answered the tortoise, looking Carlos squarely in the eye. "It would never work. Dr Funk, our creator and leader told me that, and he knows everything. He went to great lengths to surgically remove my head, all for my own good. He says melons are generally more reliable."

Carlos couldn't quite believe what he was hearing let alone seeing. He'd never seen anyone so completely brainwashed in his life before.

Muttering a swear word or two along with the words "stupid" and "nutter" Carlos strode forward and pulled the melon off the tortoise's head.

"Ow," said the tortoise. He looked high and low, giving his neck a good stretch before noticing the watermelon on the floor. After a brief panic and a moment or two of pondering the penny dropped. The realization that he had been duped by Dr Funk was evident by the sadness in his big brown eyes, which were sitting in his normal tortoise-like head. Everything he had previously believed in had been shattered.

"I still have a head."

"Yes!" exclaimed Carlos. "Now can you please let me inside my phone box? There's quite a breeze out here."

The three bizarre creatures, well two bizarre creatures and a perfectly normal tortoise, huddled together and came to a decision.

"Yes," answered the tortoise finally. "But only if we can come with you. This place isn't quite what we thought it was."

Carlos's mind began to tick. These creatures were still loyal to this "Dr Funk", or so Dr Funk thought.

"Yes. Yes you can," he replied. "But before we can leave I need you to help me with something."

* * *

Carlos had learned a lot about the evil Dr Funk from talking to the tortoise and his surgically enhanced companions. Dr Funk was an experimental[13] scientist from the nearby planet of Sandwich. He'd had a difficult childhood, having been raised in captivity between two giant slices of bread. His parents were giant slugs, and it

---

13   Emphasis on the mental

was still a mystery how Dr Funk had been born. Nevertheless, after the Year of the Great Saltstorm, the breaded shackles holding the twelve year old Ebenezer Funk were no longer replenished and he eventually ate his way to freedom.

Ebenezer's experience wasn't unique. *Children should be seen and not heard* in Sandwich, and it was common for parents to restrain naughty infants using the plentiful resource of bread.

Ebenezer was just lucky that his parents were slugs, those who were mysteriously birthed to lions rarely survived the post-pub munchies.

Anyway, Ebenezer was understandably a little perturbed by the somewhat backward culture of Sandwich, but instead of making the most of his new life of freedom he had dwelled on the past, becoming bitter and twisted and dedicating his waking hours to formulating his revenge. He fell into a life of science which resulted in the hatching of many a plan to destroy the planet, or at least the inhabitants of Sandwich.

All of which had so far failed.

Even so, the tortoise urged caution.

"For a long time Dr Funk has been talking about the Ultimate Weapon of Mass Destruction, something which he now claims he has built. I can believe it too. Recently his experiments have been increasingly successful, including the mind-control machines you have seen. You may have escaped from them, but two of your friends have been under the influence of these for days now. I wouldn't be surprised if, after years of failed attempts, he has finally managed to build a weapon capable of wreaking revenge on Sandwich."

Carlos was now starkly aware that he was dealing with

a fully deranged nutter. He wanted nothing more than to rescue his friends and get as far away as possible from Dr Funk and his Ultimate Weapon of Mass Destruction. Carlos just had one question left that he had to ask.

"If Dr Funk was so evil, why did you work for him?"

"Well..." began the tortoise, feeling a little stupid. "He was really nice to me when I first met him. He went to a lot of effort to sort out my dry throat... or at least I thought he did... and I believed his sob story. I still do actually, I have heard that the people of Sandwich are quite backward, but I doubt they deserve to be killed because of it."

"I'd agree with that," stated Carlos, sympathetic to the targeted inhabitants of Sandwich, but not so much that it would delay him from his plan to run away as quickly as possible. He had no reason to get involved in the squabbles of this world. The most important thing to him was rescuing his friends before Dr Funk cut them into pieces and added them to his ranks of mishmash servants, and this was explained wholeheartedly to the strange creatures.

For the next few hours, the tortoise and Carlos sat whispering to each other whilst trying not to let the hyperactive hyena overhear. It wouldn't be particularly helpful if Dr Funk discovered their plans thanks to hearing them screeched excitedly across the plains.

CHAPTER 13

Carlos's hands and feet were chained together, and he shuffled towards Dr Funk's evil lair led by a galah without any wings, a hyper-active hyena on springs and a tortoise with a watermelon on his head. The recently formed team had decided that in order to rescue Maria and Terrence successfully, Dr Funk must believe that the three surgically altered creatures were still under his leadership. The tortoise, Steve, had been a little bit upset about putting the watermelon back on his head, but for the good of the plan he knew he must.

Carlos was in two minds about the whole thing. Having three comrades inside Dr Funk's lair was clearly a massive advantage when trying to rescue his friends. But what if they weren't really on his side? Or what if Dr Funk managed to turn them back against him? He had only known them for about five minutes after all. Regardless of Carlos's many doubts, this was far more of a plan that he had expected to get together. And to be fair, what other options did he have?

Carlos was pretty sure he could count on Steve the

tortoise. Carlos had seen the devastation in his eyes when he had realised the lies Dr Funk had been feeding him. Steve had been really hurt. And to think he'd been walking around with that watermelon on his head for all that time, bless him. *Tortoises must be a bit slow,"* Carlos chuckled to himself[14].

Carlos hadn't quite got the same relationship with the others yet, so he was desperately hoping that Steve's leadership was enough to keep them on side. The four peculiar comrades finished their walk across the rocky desert and reached the front entrance of Dr Funk's lair, which was still locked following Carlos's escape.

"Are we ready for this?" asked Steve, in his careful and calming tortoise voice.

"Yes," affirmed Carlos. "Let's do it."

The pink hyena, Sparkles, let out an excited shriek and bounced far above the others.

"Wheeeeeeee!" he cried, before another sharp peck from the galah quietened him down.

"Sparkles!" began the tortoise, shaking his head slowly. "We really, really need you to be quiet for a while. It's really important! If you're not we will be stuck here with Dr Funk forever, and Carlos's friends will never be freed. Do you understand?"

Sparkles nodded, chastised and upset. It wasn't his fault he was full of life. What else would you expect from a pink hyena with springs on his feet? Misery and suicidal tendencies? Unlikely.

Carlos really hoped that they wouldn't regret bringing

---

14   Sorry, that was terrible but it's not my sense of humour. Carlos
     may be a stereotypical Mexican in that he is smooth,
     handsome and a hit with the ladies, but he definitely isn't
     funny.

Sparkles with them.

Steve pressed his key-card against an electronic pad on the wall, and the door opened. The four rescuers entered the lair, the door whizzing down behind them. This was it, their time had come. Carlos exchanged a knowing look with Steve, and assumed his role of captured prisoner. Head down, quiet and glum looking, he followed Steve along the pristine white corridor, towards the heart of Dr Funk's lair. The three strange creatures strutted (or bounced) along, heads held high ready for praise from their newly distrusted master, Dr Funk. They kept the act up the whole time as they didn't know when they would meet another creature.

Eventually they reached the main laboratory. As they rounded the corner, Carlos saw a grinning Dr Funk sitting on a stool behind a high desk.

"Oh no," said Steve, shaking his head glumly.

Surrounding Dr Funk was a whole squadron of guards, all strange creatures which had had bizarre additions or changes made to their bodies. Some had extra legs, some had flippers. One giant squid had a scorpion tail with a shower head attached. They would definitely qualify as a diverse group of creatures, but the one thing that they all had in common was that every single member was pointing their gun at Carlos and his accomplices.

"So, Steve," said Dr Funk. "You think that you can out-kid me do you? In case you've forgotten what I taught you, I know everything."

Steve and his downhearted comrades looked bemused. Carlos instantly suspected that he had been tricked by one of them, but there were only signs of confusion. He felt his heart sink to the bottom of his stomach.

Dr Funk was waiting for us?! How could he possibly know we were planning this? They had been careful. Even Sparkles had been quiet!

Dr Funk approached Steve and wrenched the watermelon off his head. He threw it dramatically to the floor where it smashed, seeds and pink mess flying everywhere.

Kicking pieces of watermelon aside, Dr Funk rummaged through the squelchiness and held up a small helmet similar to the ones that Carlos, Maria and Terrence had been wearing when Carlos had woken up in the laboratory.

It dawned on Carlos straight away. Dr Funk had read Steve's mind and knew all about the plan.

"Free me!" he hissed at his three comrades urgently. He wished in hindsight that they hadn't actually fastened the chains up, but when the plan had been to pretend to put Carlos into captivity they had thought this would be much better. It wouldn't really have been believable if an unrestrained Carlos had followed them into Dr Funk's lair.

Steve fumbled with the lock at turbo-tortoise speed[15], giving Dr Funk's guards ample time to completely surround the four would-be rescuers.

"To the dungeons!" commanded Dr Funk. "All of them."

---

15   A speed slightly faster than negative

CHAPTER 14

The baby cake dragon carefully picked Carlos up with one of her sponge paws and placed him on her gateaux-ed back.

"If you've any sense, you'll hold on very tightly," she advised. "I've not long learned how to fly."

"Great," muttered Carlos. "Just when it couldn't get any better..."

Carlos was quite annoyed with himself about the whole situation. After his terrible duck experience he had luckily ended up in what appeared to be a perfectly nice place, but had incurred the wrath of its inhabitants by eating it. And now he was on the back of a learner-flying dragon, waiting to be judged and most likely punished by her hill-sized parents! Carlos really wished he hadn't kidnapped those jelly babies now, it had definitely been a bad idea.

His behaviour was very much out of character. He had done many stupid things in the past which he wasn't proud of, like cheating on his girlfriend Maria, but they were due to his drinking. That was no excuse, he knew that, but to upset people when sober was new to him and he really didn't like it.

Feeling downhearted, alone and a little fearful, Carlos held on tight as the baby dragon lolloped along the ground and jumped high into the air.

The dragon flapped her wings and they jerked up higher and higher with each stroke.

"I'm doing it! I'm flying!" cried the cake dragon. Her obvious amazement that she was still airborne wasn't making Carlos feel any better.

Just as they seemed to be gaining some decent height the flapping stopped. Carlos heard a piercing little dragon shriek as they started to fall sharply to the ground. The cake dragon landed with a little "squelch" and lay still for a moment. Carlos rolled off her back and bounced a few times before coming to a halt.

"I'm sorry!" wheezed the dragon, looking sheepishly towards the floor. "But I did say I've not long learned how to fly! And it's loads more difficult with someone watching!"

Carlos rubbed his elbow which was a little sore from the whole experience. Thankful that the floor was made of bouncy candy floss he tried to calm the cake dragon. It was about time he started being nice Carlos again after all. "Don't worry! I'm ok, the fall didn't hurt and you nearly had it there! But is there not any other way we can travel instead of flying?"

"I'm afraid not," answered the dragon. "I can't fit along the roads and bridges the jelly babies have made, I'd end up squashing them!"

Carlos could see this, he himself was so much bigger than the jelly babies that he could easily crush everything. The cake dragon would likely destroy whole streets with one footstep. "I understand. Well don't worry. This time I won't watch, I'll keep my eyes firmly shut."

The cake dragon smiled and looked a little more relaxed.

Reluctantly, Carlos climbed across her back and held on tightly to a large glacé cherry. He shut his eyes, not because he'd promised to but because he was petrified.

The cake dragon took another juddering run-up and jumped, high into the air. Carlos could feel them slowly rising upwards with each flap of the cake dragon's wings. He prepared himself for another fall but it never came.

Carlos braved it and opened his eyes. He gasped in astonishment. He could see for miles and miles, surely almost to the end of Pink River. Past the sheer pink cliffs, which lay beyond the rolling meadows and township he had just been in, was a bubbling yellow sea from which waves erupted and fizzed along a rocky beach. Looking in the direction they were flying, Carlos could see that they were getting much closer to the two cake mountains that the dragon had pointed out as her parents.

"It's beautiful," Carlos said. "What a view!"

The cake dragon looked around at Carlos, a horrified look on her face.

"You said you wouldn't look!" she cried, suddenly lurching downwards, losing control.

"I'm not! I'm not looking!" he shouted as they spiralled towards the floor.

He closed his eyes as he saw a pink meadow quickly dominating his vision.

The cake dragon hit the candy floss floor and bounced, high above the top of the mountains. Flapping her wings frantically, she regained her balance and turned upright again before landing and skidding along a path, right into the side of a huge multi-coloured mountain.

The mountain opened a huge, gleaming, yellow eye.

"Still not mastered landing yet my little Éclair?" asked Dad in a deep gruff voice. The mountain stretched out a large chocolatey wing and yawned widely.

"At least you haven't woken me up quite so early today," he said. "Next time though, hold your wings steady and glide in. You don't need to flap, it's much easier to control your landing if you don't."

"Thanks Daddy," said Éclair the baby cake dragon, who had slowly picked herself up from her splat-landing.

A large eye blinked at Carlos. "So, who's this then?" asked the Daddy cake dragon, his voice booming around the Cake Mountains.

"I wonder if all of these mountains are dragons?" thought Carlos, suddenly aware that there could be twenty, even thirty of these dragons around.

"I found him in Pink River," said Éclair. "He's **not** been very nice!"

"Really?" replied the dragon. "Well I'm glad you brought him to us then, Éclair. Well done."

The dragon turned his head to one side and nudged the mountain next to him.

"Pastry," he whispered soothingly. "Our daughter has been busy this morning already."

There was a faint murmuring and yawning, before a groggy looking female dragon woke up next to him.

"Morning Custard," she slurred. Her red lined éclair lips smiled at him, struggling with the words in her drowsiness.

She nuzzled in towards him, and opened her big yellow eyes. She was going to pay attention to her daughter even if it was a struggle this morning.

"Hello Éclair," she smiled. "You're up bright and early. So what have you been up to this morning then?"

"Hi Mummy," Éclair replied. Carlos couldn't help but admire the bond between the three dragons. It was obvious they were a very tightly knit family.

"I found him in the village Mummy! He's been eating the houses and kidnapping the jelly babies! He was going to eat them as well!!"

"Oh no," soothed Pastry, "not another one. We've had a few of these recently haven't we?"

"Yes Mummy. I don't like them. Why do they have to be so mean?! Don't they realise the jellies are my friends?"

"I don't think they do, dear. They probably don't even know that the jelly babies have friends. I think that in their world they eat jelly babies. You know, like we eat the rock animals? In their world they might be friends with rock animals hadn't they? And then they would be sad if we ate them."

"Yes, I suppose so Mummy," Éclair sighed. She scrunched up her strawberry jam-covered lips and glanced at the sky, deep in thought. "But what are we to do? He can't be allowed to eat them or their houses."

Carlos was watching quietly. He had a feeling that Pastry the Mummy dragon would be more sympathetic to him than he had thought. He didn't want to ruin that with his ill-thought out words.

"Hmmm… I don't know." Pastry looked at Carlos. "Did you know that the jelly babies were Éclair's friends?"

Carlos shook his head. "No, I didn't. I'm really sorry Éclair."

"I think," continued Pastry in her soft kindly voice, "that we should give him one more chance, because he didn't know. Shall we teach him about what he is allowed to eat, and what he is not? And then," Pastry looked at Carlos, a clear warning in her stare, "if he breaks the rules once more, we will punish him."

"Hmmmm…" pondered Éclair, tilting her head so far that it looked like a wobbling vanilla slice would slide off onto the floor. "I suppose that would be fair."

"Thanks so much!" blurted Carlos. "I will behave, I promise!" A fierce stare from Pastry silenced him, but her face mellowed as she looked back towards her daughter.

"Éclair, why don't you take him back to the Jelly Village? He will apologise to the jelly babies, with you translating of course, and then you can show him around and tell him what he is, and isn't, allowed to eat."

"Yes Mummy!" answered Éclair excitedly. "I can do that!"

"And Éclair," sighed Pastry the Mummy cake dragon. "Please try not to drop this one on the way."

CHAPTER 15

"Over there are candy canes," explained Éclair the cake dragon, pointing at a ploughed field with lots of pink and white striped items protruding from the ground. "You can eat them, although you have to buy them from the farmer who grows them first."

Carlos nodded, he had had quite an education this morning from Éclair. She was adamant that he would know every single item in the land that he was allowed to eat, and more importantly, not eat.

Carlos was trying his hardest to remember it all too. He liked Éclair and her parents, and it was his fault they had got off on the wrong foot. He felt very guilty about his actions and felt he should make some effort towards the local inhabitants. This had already started with the translated apology he had made to the jelly babies earlier.

That hadn't gone too well.

The jelly babies had gathered in their droves at the edge of the village, waving their pitchforks in the air and screaming their unfathomable language at him. Carlos didn't want to ask Éclair what it meant, in fact he was pretty sure an eight year old dragon wouldn't, and shouldn't, know the vocabulary they were using.

They had quietened down a little when he began to speak, his speech delivered via Éclair's translation.

"Hi everyone," he began. "Thank you all for gathering here to listen to me. I'm afraid I owe you a huge apology. I didn't think about my actions when I ate your houses, to me they were just food…"

That incomplete sentence in particular went down badly, and Carlos didn't attempt to finish it such were the roars that greeted Éclair's translation.

"I was famished having not eaten for a couple of days, and I'm afraid I am not up to scratch with your local customs. I will learn though, and Éclair has promised to fill me in so that I will not make the same mistakes again."

Carlos waited for a couple of seconds whilst Éclair finished translating before carrying on with his speech.

"I apologise in particular to the inhabitants of the Jelly Village whom I trapped in my top pocket. I promise you that I wasn't going to eat you, and I will never do such a thing again. If there is anything I can do to make this up to you, then please tell Éclair."

At the mention of his pocket, a riot almost broke out. Some jelly babies had brought things to throw at Carlos, and they rained on him now. One had even brought their front door, and this was launched at Carlos by a group of angry men. Carlos was dismayed that his apology had gone so badly, and it took all of his self-control not to flippantly pick up the chocolate front door and eat it.

Still, he didn't and he **had** tried. He had meant every word he had said. Carlos was truly sorry and he would make an effort to repair the gingerbread houses if the jelly babies would let him. There was no chance of that at the moment, and he guessed he couldn't blame them. If the boot had been on the other foot, he wouldn't have given the time of day to a strange creature that had eaten half of his home town. Carlos knew it would be some time before he got any less than an angry reception around the Jelly Village, but he could tell that Éclair appreciated his efforts.

Following the attempted apology, Éclair had taken him away for his culinary tour of Pink River. They had seen the town, the waterfalls, the farmlands and the wetlands.

Carlos was amazed at how little he was allowed to eat.

"I'm not even allowed to eat this pink rock?"

"No!" said Éclair. "That's part of the waterfall! The river might get diverted if you eat that, and then you'll flood the Jelly Village."

"What about this?" he asked, scooping a handful of toffee out of the bottom of the river.

"No," said Éclair. "If you eat that, the fish will have nothing to eat! You can eat the fish though."

"I can't eat the fish, Éclair. They are made of coal! It will kill me!"

"Too bad," said Eclair. "You can eat the grass then, that will grow back."

Carlos bit his lip and didn't argue. He was sure they'd find more food for him at some point. He could eat candy floss for now, but he wasn't sure quite how long his insides would last if that proved to be his staple diet.

It had taken ages, but Éclair finally declared that they had seen everything Carlos was allowed to eat in the Jelly Village and its surroundings.

"If there's anything you're unsure about though Carlos," she clarified, "just don't eat it. You can ask me about it when you next see me."

Carlos reassured her that he would, and lay down for a hard-earned rest. He'd had a hard day or two and he was desperate to relax and take stock of things for a while.

"What do you think you're doing?" asked Éclair. "You can't rest now! It's play time!"

"Oh Éclair," Carlos groaned, "I'm too tired, I've walked for miles. I can't play right now..."

Éclair was quite patient for an eight year old, and Carlos had almost five minutes rest before she threw him on her back and flew them both back towards the Cake Mountains.

CHAPTER 16

No further away than the width of a greasy pimpled teenager's skin, but actually in a completely different dimension called $E=mc^2$, a pink hyena with springs on its feet, a tortoise, a galah with no wings and the other existence of Carlos were being led down a spiral staircase into the depths of the Earth. Eventually, they got to the bottom and Dr Funk's strangely adapted guards threw them into a putrid and damp cell, which already had occupants.

"Carlos?!" shouted Maria, throwing herself at him in a warm embrace. "What are you doing here?"

"It was full at the Hilton," said a winking Carlos.

"No, really?" laughed Maria. "I have no idea where we are!"

"Me neither," admitted Carlos. "We came to rescue you but it went a little wrong..."

He gave Terrence a warm hug too. He knew Maria's brother well from over the years.

The guard's footsteps and squeaking frames faded

away with the candlelight, and the cell grew darker and darker.

"I don't like the dark!!" screeched the hyena, shifting uneasily from foot to foot.

"Don't worry, we'll look after you," Maria said kindly, grasping Sparkles's paw and looking straight into his wide eyes. This calmed Sparkles a little. Maria had one of those extremely warm smiles which exudes confidence and makes you feel like you've known someone for years, even if you've never met before. "But I'm afraid you'll have to get used to it. It will be properly dark soon, and then we'll have no light until the guards come with their candles again."

"Owhhh!" wept the hyena, his nervousness causing him to bounce, hit the ceiling and ricochet around the room. Eventually he crashed into a stoic Steve the tortoise and slumped on the ground.

"I think you should stay lying down for now," recommended Steve. "This is going to be terrible..." he groaned.

"Carlos, who are your friends?" asked Maria. She sat next to Sparkles, patting and reassuring him as much as she could.

With an apology for not having done so already, Carlos introduced Steve the tortoise, Sparkles the pink hyena and Gladys the wing-less galah to Maria and Terrence.

The friends caught up, telling each other their stories about how they'd arrived in Dr Funk's dungeon. Maria and Terrence were confused but nowhere near as confused as Carlos was. He couldn't remember how he had got there at all!

"Well I know why that is," said Maria. "You were drunk again."

Carlos looked at her, unable to remember.

"I don't think I was..." he began.

"You were!" she snapped. "You left me a voicemail!"

Carlos was stumped, he couldn't remember anything. He couldn't even remember a hangover. He knew better than to argue though so he mumbled an apology and sat quietly, wracking his brains.

The others sat around in awkward silence, apart from Steve who chuntered away to himself.

"I'm glad you're here though," said Terrence. "You'll help us get out of here won't you?"

"Of course I will," replied Carlos, hoping that this telephone box Terrence and Maria had arrived in would be really useful and take them back too.

Maria stood up and stumbled across the room. She might be annoyed with Carlos, but she was still very glad he was here. Tripping over Steve on the way, she sat down next to Carlos and rested her head on his shoulder.

"I wish we had some light," she said. "It's awfully depressing in here without it."

"Hang on a sec!" shouted Carlos triumphantly, her words sparking a memory.

Reaching into the mysterious satchel he couldn't remember acquiring, he rummaged around amongst the scientific equipment until he found the torch he had taken off Dr Funk's workbench.

"And the Lord said, let there be..."

Carlos shook and tapped the torch in frustration.

"Shoot. The batteries must have gone."

He tried again anyway. There was a squeal from

Gladys. "Turn that off! Don't point it at me!!" She squawked frantically, trying to flap wings that weren't there.

"It is turned off!" laughed Carlos. "Don't worry!"

"What's turned off?" asked Maria.

It was pitch black and no-one else could see the torch that Carlos was waving around.

"Gladys?" he asked tentatively. "Can you see in the dark? And if not, how did you know I was pointing something at you?"

"It hurts!" screamed Gladys, clearly still in some distress. "Dr Funk uses it to torture me! Keep it away from me, please!!"

Carlos pointed the torch at his hand in curiosity and felt a strong burning sensation. He pulled his hand away quickly, blowing on it to cool it down.

What on Earth had he found?!

CHAPTER 17

The prisoners sat in the darkness, discussing the strange torch which Carlos had stolen from Dr Funk.

"So he used to burn you with it every day?" asked Maria, sympathetically yet incredulously.

"Yes..." shook Gladys, who was obviously uncomfortable with even talking about it. "For a few hours every day. He said it was making me stronger."

"Stronger?" asked Terrence. "But you're a chicken with no wings. You can't even have biceps!"

"I'm a galah!" squawked Gladys. "You won't be warned again, we're completely different! How many talking chickens do you know?!"

Terrence was confused. He'd never known that tortoises or hyenas could talk, ·but he had spoken to some colourful chickens in the zoo, and had whole conversations with them about someone called "Pretty Polly" before.

Gladys got back to the subject of Dr Funk's abuse of her with the burning torch. "Anyway, he meant I was getting stronger on the inside, not the outside. I don't feel it though, in fact quite the opposite. Every time he used that thing on me it felt like I was losing part of my soul. My memories, my purpose, even my day to day thoughts felt like they were slipping away. It was horrible!"

Maria placed her hand on Gladys's claw. "Thanks for sharing this with us Gladys, it must be really difficult for you. Everything's going to be alright, I promise you."

Carlos had been listening, but he was slightly distracted by the torch. He was always fascinated by new gadgets, and this one in particular was giving him some ideas.

"I'm gonna try pointing it at the prison bars," he said. "I think it could burn them for us."

The others agreed that it was a good idea, although he could tell Gladys was a bit sceptical about using the torch for any reason. The prison bars were wooden, and if even one of them could be set on fire then that would at least allow the humans to squeeze out.

Carlos pointed the torch at the middle bar and held it steady for a while. A faint odour eventually filled the cell and the prisoners began to get excited.

"It's burning!" Maria cried. "We're gonna get out of here!"

The prisoners all stepped backwards to allow Carlos as much space as he could. If they were really lucky, there would be flames soon and they would have some light to help them pick out an escape route.

If they had had seats, the prisoners would have been right on the edge of them for about ten minutes before anyone spoke again.

"I don't think it's doing any good," said Carlos, a flat resignation in his voice.

Turning the torch off, Carlos moved closer to the bars and put his hand out tentatively to touch the one he had been trying to burn.

There was a loud "Mee-yaw!!!"[16] as Carlos touched the wooden bar. Carlos yelped and jumped away from it.

"Are you ok?" asked Maria. "Did it burn you? Come here, let me have a look."

"No, no, I'm fine," said Carlos, his voice wavering. "But as crazy as it sounds, I think it bit me."

Carlos cursed as he tripped over the snoring Sparkles and landed in the tangle of legs, springs and feathers on the floor of the prison cell.

"It bit you?" asked Terrence. "But it's a piece of wood, don't be stupid!" It wasn't very often that Terrence felt intellectually superior to someone, and if they had been able to see him, they'd have seen a huge smug grin across his face.

"It did, I swear!" said Carlos. "If you don't believe me, go and touch it yourself!"

Terrence was unsure. His head was telling him it was impossible, but Carlos wasn't stupid. Why would he say such a silly thing? The prison cell bar was an inanimate object[17]. It couldn't have bitten Carlos, surely?

Terrence approached the bars and put his hand out tentatively.

"It's ok," he said, withdrawing his shaking hand. "I believe you."

He didn't believe Carlos, but he wasn't sure and he was far too scared to touch the bar himself. As usual, his bold sister Maria stepped up, nervously but bravely

---

16   A screeching cross between a mew and an "ee-yaw"
17   Much like Terrence's brain

running her hand along the prison cell bars.

One solid bar. Two solid bars. Three solid bars. Maria was getting confident. Four solid bars. A gap. A gap! Could they get free?!

Maria whispered excitedly. "Carlos! It's gone! There's a gap in the bars, I think I can get out!"

The others started to chatter excitedly, and there was the sound of an excited hyena bouncing and screeching around the cell. Maria slipped between the bars, into the dark confines of the outer prison.

Carlos was pleased that they were able to get out of the cell, but his mind was racing. If the cell bar had disappeared without actually burning properly, then what on earth was that torch he had found? And where *was* that thing that had bitten him?!

They prisoners groped their way through the darkness towards the hole in the bars, and one by one snuck through with the exception of Steve the tortoise.

"Typical," he moaned, feeling sorry for himself. "I don't fit. As usual, nothing goes right for me. Don't worry though, you go. I'll be happy rotting here for all eternity."

"Guys!" Carlos hissed. "Steve can't get out! If we wait a few minutes I can use the torch on another bar and we can all escape."

Everyone was in agreement and they stayed close together as Carlos pointed the torch at another bar.

"Do you think it's worked?" asked Maria after a while. "We can't actually see whether it's gone or not and it seems like an awfully long time!"

The same strange burning odour the previous bar had given out had been around for a while, but like the first bar there were no flames. Carlos tentatively put his hand out and felt around.

"It's still there," he confirmed as he touched warm, soft wood. If he didn't know better he could have sworn it wriggled under his touch. "It feels as if it's nearly done though. We'll give it another couple of minutes and it might disappear like the other one."

The prisoners waited silently, and a short while later they heard a "POP!" followed by a fast rustling away from them.

"Did you hear that?" asked Terrence. "Do you think that means it's gone?"

Carlos switched the torch off and put his hand out.

"It's gone!" he proclaimed triumphantly, waving around at thin air. "Come on Steve, let's get out of here!"

There was a wittering of excitement amongst the prisoners, and one by one they squeezed between the bars and out of the cell, all grasping onto each other in the darkness.

As they made their way across the dungeon, hopefully towards the steps they had come down they heard a loud shriek.

"Mee-yaw!"

The sound echoed eerily around the dungeon.

"Mee-yaw!" they heard again.

"Was... was that cry from the same creature or are there two of them?" asked Terrence, his voice shaking as he said what the others were all thinking.

"I don't know," conceded Carlos, "but I don't want to hang around and find out! Come on everyone!"

Pulling Steve the tortoise along as quickly as they could, the prisoners located the stairs and started their ascent towards freedom.

Matty Millard

CHAPTER 18

In the Cake Mountains of Pink River, Carlos had spent the afternoon living a stark reminder of his duck-related nightmare, this time avoiding the stomping feet of baby cake dragons during a frightening game of tag.

Éclair had made him join in. "It is part of making up your nastiness," she explained.

Carlos's protests had fallen on deaf ears, but he wasn't quite sure, given his relative size to the dragons, what he could really offer to the game. He flailed around the field, diving out of the way of giant footsteps and falling dragons.

After more than a few near-death experiences, a physically intact but mentally scarred Carlos felt that he had probably paid enough penance for one day. Some of the dragons had started to get distracted and one by one had wandered off to play at other things. Carlos took the opportunity to do the same and he ran off to recover in a nearby field.

Once he had caught his breath, he remembered the satchel he had found but had not yet had time to have a proper look through.

Excitedly, he pulled out a bound leather folder, worn and tatty but clearly well loved. He had already seen enough of the insides of the satchel to know there was some kind of scientific contraption in there, and he was intrigued. Physics was a love of his, and the possibility that something might bring him back a semblance of normality was comforting.

He opened the folder carefully, and pored over the handwritten scrawl inside. Carlos smiled, it was proper scientist's handwriting. On the title page was printed "Is There Intelligent Life Beyond Utopia?" After flicking through a few pages it was clear that this was essentially a research bible into the workings of inter-dimensional travel and the places the author, Dr Oliver Oliver[18], had seen.

Carlos's spirits were lifted instantly. *Is this what has happened to me? Does this mean that somewhere in here it will tell me how I can get home?!* Carlos knew straight away that he'd be spending at least the next couple of hours reading through the rest of the manuscript.

By the time he had finished reading, Carlos had a clear knowledge of how to travel between dimensions. There was even a small contraption, which Dr Oliver[2] referred to as "The WorldChanger", inside the satchel which allowed him to do so! He folded the strange metal device out to reveal a wobbly looking tripod with some strong looking clamps attached, and a small keypad at the top of the frame. He could travel around! There was a chance he could get home!

Unfortunately there was no mention in the folder of

---

18   Or Dr Oliver[2] (squared) as he wittily referred to himself

any dimension which sounded like his home. One place had taken his fancy though, there was a description of a lovely sounding dimension where intelligent life forms did exist, some of which sounded like they might be humans. The fact that it was referred to as the Kingdom of Happiness and All Things Warm and Fluffy did help to sell the place too. Carlos quite liked Pink River and the cake dragons however, so he was in no rush to leave right away. He was sure that he would be gracing the Kingdom of Happiness and All Things Warm and Fluffy with his presence soon enough.

Contented, he looked up as Éclair bounded squishily over. Fearing for his life again, Carlos was lifted up onto her back and he held on tightly as they flew back to her parents for tea.

CHAPTER 19

A greasy teenager was frantically stuffing his football kit into his bag, he was going to be late for the bus to school. It was games this afternoon, the highlight of his week. Today would be no different, he would play football and probably win. However, this game was more important that most, and he had no idea that it would change the course of history forever.

The two giant pimples on his face were now so large, so tightly packed with custard and so closely pressed together, that it was inevitable his afternoon exercise would shake them into joining as one.

As I'm sure you remember, these two pimples were in fact dimensions. They were already so near to merging that Carlos was living simultaneously in both of them. Their inter-dimensional membranes were so closely squeezed together that some of the trees at the edge of Dr Funk's lair were blossoming candy canes due to a rare phenomenon known as inter-dimensional confectional osmosis[19].

The events about to occur on our greasy teenager's face meant that the two Carlos's and the dimensions they existed in had only a few hours before they became one.

---

19   This phenomenon can, on occasion, cause some quite serious side-effects. The worst known example was the penetration of the dimensional membrane of Dimension One by a giant living butter toffee. This butter toffee was one of the rare kind which roams the land consuming everything it touches, growing as it eats. Unfortunately, Dimension One was diabetic, and the presence of a growing living butter toffee was just too much. Dimension One became rushed and over-energetic. Life inside it became too fast paced and too high pressure. The dimension was bursting at the seams, the dimensional membrane stretching and straining to keep itself intact. Eventually the whole dimension exploded, taking with it fourteen neighbouring dimensions and a small signpost to a public toilet, kindly commissioned by Puddled, the God of Dodgy and Unclean Alleyways.

CHAPTER 20

There was a loud "Mee-yaw!" and the fleeing prisoners froze.

"Come on!" Carlos encouraged, pulling Maria's hand to hurry her up the stairs. She passed this along the line, all the way to the back where Steve was trying his best to ascend at faster than tortoise speed.

"Ow," said Steve loudly. "Ow. Ow. And ow again."

"What's the matter Steve?" called back Maria.

"Well," Steve began. "You know Carlos thought he got bitten earlier? I think he was right."

"I told you!" said Carlos. "But why's that?"

"Well there is definitely a pair of teeth clamped around my leg right now," said Steve in his usual deadpan voice. "It's quite painful you know."

"Why didn't you say so?!" shouted Carlos, running down the steps to Steve where he quickly saw the problem. The light had improved as they got closer to the top, so Carlos could see the faint outline of Steve who had got a strange snake-like creature wrapped around, and chewing on, his leg.

Carlos kicked the snake.

"Ow," said Steve, again. "Don't kick it, it makes his teeth dig in more."

Carlos tried pulling the snake off but had no luck. He let go in pain, and looked at his hands. Splinters!! The snake was made of wood!

"Let me try," offered the onlooking Gladys.

She pecked the snake viciously, causing it to hiss and uncurl. Rising up into an aggressive stance, the wooden snake flickered its tongue at Gladys and wavered in front of her, staring. Gladys shrank back, fearful.

After a moment or two of looking at Gladys, the snake stopped hissing. Eventually it lowered itself to floor level, and appeared at peace.

"Well done Gladys!" cried Carlos. "Let's go!"

Maria dropped back to Steve, fussing around him and encouraging him onwards.

"Carlos," said Steve. "That weird snake thing is following us."

Carlos turned. Sure enough, the creature was slithering up the steps just a couple of paces behind Steve.

"Try and ignore it," said Carlos. "Just walk as fast as you can."

They did until Steve moaned again.

"Carlos, it's overtaken me now."

Gladys cried out in shock. The wooden snake had leapt onto her and curled up around her leg, her head resting on her back.

"Carlos! It's on me now!" she called. "It's not biting though," she said slowly, a little unsure about the whole situation.

There was a second "Mee-yaw!" sound from the

bottom of the stairs, and a rustling. Before they knew it there was a second snake wrapped around Gladys's other leg. Both snakes seemed at ease with Gladys though, there was no aggression or biting, and they just lay with their heads resting on her back.

Gladys confirmed she was fine to carry on, so concerned but unable to shift the snakes, the prisoners climbed the stairs. Carlos and Maria reached the top first, and peered around the doorway. The light made their eyes hurt, so they were forced to squint until they got used to the brightness. By the time the others reached the top they could see properly. It was time to escape.

"Oh. So this is where the dungeons are," said Steve. "I always wondered what this door was."

Carlos stared at him, an expression of disbelief on his face.

"I thought you knew the way around?" he questioned. "That was quite an important part of our plan. How were we going to rescue my friends if Dr Funk hadn't led us to the dungeons?"

"I knew he would," beamed the tortoise.

The plan they had entered Dr Funk's lair with had never had any chance of working. Carlos was more than a little frustrated, but Maria knew him well and gave him a gentle nudge. Calmness was needed now if they were to escape.

"Ok," conceded Carlos. "So which way is the best way out Steve?"

"Left. If we go right it takes us right back into the middle of his lair."

"No!" interrupted Gladys. "It's left towards the lair and right to the Eastern Corridor. We need to go right!"

"Whooohooooo!!" helped Sparkles at the top of his voice. "We're esscaaapiiiing!!"

There was no further discussion about the direction they must take, the sight of Sparkles bounding down the corridor without them made their mind up straight away.

Left it was. Sparkles could sod off. They didn't know where they were, and a bouncing, screeching pink hyena was an excellent decoy.

CHAPTER 21

Sparkles the pink hyena bounced along the corridor, giggling hysterically at the escape he was part of.

He looked behind to see where the others were, crashed into a wall and collapsed in a heap on the ground.

Panting, he sat up and waited.

Where are they? he asked himself a few minutes later. He knew that he was fast – his springs always meant that he bounded away from people quickly, but he had only come down one corridor so they should have caught up by now.

Concerned, he bounced as lightly as he could back to the start of the corridor and peered around the corner. He was just in time to see them disappearing out of view at the other end.

Where are they going? They knew he had come this way – how couldn't they with the amount of noise he made?

It dawned on him that they were leaving him behind, and he sank to the floor. His eyes grew large and round, and slowly filled with tears.

"Why don't they want me?!" he wailed. Sparkles knew he could be loud and annoying, but he didn't think he was that bad...

After a moment or two of weeping, Sparkles pulled himself together and sat up. Sparkles wasn't one to give up without trying, he could catch them up easily and escape too. He didn't want to get stuck here with the evil Dr Funk!

Besides, he knew that they were heading right back into the middle of Dr Funk's lair and he had to stop them.

* * *

Carlos led the way along the corridor, stopping to peer around every corner before giving the all-clear. Maria fussed alongside her brother and tried to keep a close eye on everyone. Every now and then they waited for Steve the tortoise and Gladys, the galah with her new wood snake additions, to catch up. The wood snakes seemed calm and at ease with Gladys, and she didn't seem bothered by them in the slightest. Carlos had been thinking hard about this. He wasn't sure, but was it just possible that they had been the prison cell bars? The second bar had been quite warm and squidgy after he'd used the torch on it. And if they were, maybe creatures burned by the torch were somehow drawn together? The more he thought about it the more it made sense, but still he didn't mention it to anyone, it was a pretty weird theory.

As there wasn't really a plan, it didn't matter too much when Carlos peered around the next corner and saw Dr Funk busy in his laboratory, filling up jars with a strange yellow ointment he had mixed.

"I thought you said it was this way?" Terrence asked Steve, accusing the tortoise for his poor sense of direction.

"I'm sorry," he asked glumly. "It's been a long time since I came down here."

"It's been a long time since you did anything isn't it? You're so bloody slow..." Terrence had a very short temper when he was frightened.

Carlos stepped in and calmed the situation.

"It doesn't matter, we'll just turn around and go the other way. No harm done! And at least we know where Dr Funk is now."

Steve hung his head, sorry to have let his new friends down.

"I did say you should have left me."

"Don't be silly!" laughed Maria, always able to look on the bright side. "There's nothing lost, only a few minutes. At least we know we're definitely going the right way now!"

The prisoners turned around to head back past the dungeons and on to freedom when they heard a familiar sound.

"Sssssstooooooopppp!!!" screamed Sparkles as he bounded down the corridor. "Yooouuuu'rre going the wroooong wayyyyyyyyy!!"

"Run!" cried Carlos, all of sudden wishing they had followed the noisy hyena. It was surely only a matter of time before they saw their friend Dr Funk once more. They had got almost as far as the door of the dungeon when Dr Funk caught up.

There was a part of Carlos that wished they hadn't waited for the slow ones, and he had just taken Maria and Terrence to safety. After all, he'd only known the others for two minutes.

But they had put their permanently flawed existences at risk for him and his friends so he should be grateful. Come to think of it so had Sparkles, the hyena they had recently abandoned. *I reckon I owe him one,* thought Carlos, *if we ever get out of here. Maybe I could do something with those springs? I must be able to at least dampen them so that Sparkles can walk normally when he wants to…*

Carlos put those thoughts to the back of his mind for now, they had to escape before anything like that was possible.

The group stopped their fleeing when they saw Dr Funk pointing a strange looking gun at them. It was shiny and silver, with peculiar dials and flashing lights all over it. *Most probably, it has lots of different modes,* Carlos speculated. *One for firing octopus tentacles at you, one for screaming insults at people, one for turning people into purple leopards, and maybe even one for regulation shooting? Who knows, it's a crazy world?*

Carlos wasn't sure he actually wanted to find out what the gun could do, so he reluctantly put his hands in the air to show surrender. The others followed suit, even Gladys the wingless galah whose evil wood snakes circled upwards as if they were arms.

As they were escorted back towards the dungeons by Dr Funk and his bodyguards, the football playing teenager was cynically tripped and landed heavily on the floor. Somehow the referee didn't even give a foul! Despite the heavy landing which caused his two pimples to merge into one massive one, thus changing the structure of two entire dimensions, the game continued with the fans hurling abuse at the stricken official.

Matty Millard

CHAPTER 22

Carlos and Éclair the cake dragon came hurtling down through the roof of the laboratory and crash-landed next to Dr Funk, who was standing pointing a wriggling pink salmon at Maria. Around him were three potted venus fly-traps, two mangy looking wolf-dogs, a frightened cat and a goat with a very posh beard.

The frightened cat bounded away with a squeal, the wolf-dogs racing in pursuit. Sparkles breathed a huge sigh of relief and came out of hiding behind Steve. The venus fly-traps all tried to eat the same buzzing fly simultaneously, and started French-kissing passionately in front of everyone. The goat said "baa."

"What just happened?" asked Maria.

"Maria!" shouted Carlos. "What are you doing here?!"

Maria looked at Terrence for some kind of reassurance, but he was just standing there with an even more gormless look on his face than usual. It seemed that the insane events of the previous few seconds had finally blown his tiny little mind.

Éclair lifted Carlos down from her back and he ran

over to hug Maria.

"So haven't you missed me?" he asked feigning upset.

"Erm. Well no..?" Maria said. "Not really. You've been here for days."

"No I haven't!" Carlos laughed. "We were flying over Pink River just a few seconds ago, and all of a sudden we appeared here!"

"Pink River? Where's that?" asked Steve the tortoise. "I don't like pink but it sounds better than here. I hate it here."

"Well I guess it must be in a different dimension. Quite how I've travelled again I don't know, but that must be it," said Carlos coolly.

Carlos's thorough studying of Dr Oliver[2]'s manual meant that he understood the concepts behind travelling to different dimensions. The Carlos who had existed here must have swapped places with him due to inter-dimensional balancing, which would explain why he didn't remember having seen Maria. Carlos told the others what he had learned about inter-dimensional travel, and by the end of it they all had an idea about what had happened.

"That would explain where the guards have gone!" screeched Sparkles, still laughing at the smooching venus-fly traps whose actions were starting to get rather raunchy. Terrence didn't know where to look and shifted uncomfortably from foot to foot.

Little did they know that Carlos hadn't actually changed dimensions, but that two dimensions had merged together meaning that one Carlos had ceased to exist.

Incidentally, the merging of these two dimensions on the

teenager's face created one hell of a ginormous pimple. The pressure inside this gloriously gigantic specimen of acne was so great, that every time the boy moved a little too quickly a sharp throbbing rippled across his face and down his neck. Fortunately, he's one of these kids that won't pop spots. Can you imagine what *that* would have done to Carlos and his friends? He prefers them to gently explode due to natural causes and then leaves them to ooze freely so that he doesn't have to mess around with squeezing the dregs out.

Now it has been widely discussed and there are three schools of thought on what happens should a dimension explode inside of another. The first is that the void left by the departing debris slowly but surely sucks the fabric on which everything is formed back inside itself[20]. In this case, that would mean that the exploding pimple would result in the slow implosion of every dimension in existence into the boy's face. That's a whole lot of pain. The second would result in everything in the dimension getting covered in custard. The third school of thought is a rubbish school and they don't know the answer. This does however mean, that in all probability, they are the least likely to be wrong.

---

20   In case of interest, the fabric on which everything is formed is sugar paper. A useful fact in a pub quiz

Matty Millard

CHAPTER 23

Once Maria and Terrence had finished catching up with the new Carlos and had re-introduced the whole group, Éclair the cake dragon, despite being the youngest member of the team, came up with a very sensible question.

"Maria?" she asked, her Éclair eyebrows squashed together in a serious frown, "this man who kidnapped you, Dr Funk, where has he gone?"

Everyone gasped and looked around anxiously, they had forgotten all about him in the excitement. Dr Funk must still be lurking around somewhere. After Carlos and Éclair had flown in through the roof, he had been standing there, holding a fish, looking just as confused as anyone else about the seemingly rnmdao events of the previous minute. But during the discussions that followed, he must have snuck away.

"Well I vote that we take our chance and get out of here while we can," said Carlos. "If he's half as crazy as you say he is, we should jump into that phone box of yours right away!"

The group agreed wholeheartedly. Carlos persuaded them all to get onto Éclair's back as it would be much quicker than walking.

Gliding out of the hole in the roof of Dr Funk's lair, there was a synchronised gasp. The whole landscape had changed completely! Instead of the dry dusty plains of before, there were springy pink candy floss ones. A gushing yellow fizzy river flowed out into the distance.

"I hate flying," moaned Steve, who was sitting on top of Sparkles in case the hyena got over excited and jumped off in mid-flight.

"We'd never have got across that new river without it though," answered Maria.

"I know," said Steve, "but it's just so high…"

"Carlos," said Éclair quietly. "I can't see my parents anywhere…"

Carlos gazed in amazement at the scenery. Contrary to Pink River, the whole landscape was very flat. It was actually very similar to how $E=mc^2$ had been, except for the fact it was now made of confectionery. The gigantic cake dragons Pastry and Custard would have stood out for miles.

"Nor can I, Éclair," said Carlos, "but don't you worry, we'll go for a good explore soon to find them. Can we stop at the phone box first though, to drop my friends off?"

Maria spotted the phone box down below, and Éclair started her juddering but vastly improved descent.

"You're getting good at that," praised Carlos after a fairly gentle splat-landing. He led the way over to the phone box.

"Right," said Carlos, taking charge as usual. "We're

going to the Kingdom of Happiness and all Things Warm and Fluffy. It sounds like everyone is really friendly there. You guys get in and type in the following number. I'll see you at the top of Unicorn Mountain. It sounds like the best place for us to meet, apparently you can't miss it."

Carlos leafed through the folder of research until he found the page for "The Kingdom of Happiness and All Things Warm and Fluffy. The number is..."

"Hang on a minute!" cried Maria. "Aren't you coming with us?"

"Yeah I'm coming," re-assured Carlos, "but I've gotta go help Éclair find her parents first. Don't worry, I'll catch you up. I've got my own machine." He lifted up the contraption he had found in Dr Oliver[2]'s satchel.

He leaned in close to Maria and whispered. "Besides, if we can't find Éclair's parents, she won't fit in the phone box. I'll have to travel with her anyway."

"I don't want to go without you, Carlos. What if something happens and you can't get there?"

The other creatures looked a little shifty, all a bit worried about what they would do without their leader Carlos.

"Don't worry, I'll see you there I promise. Anyway, you've gotta go with these lot. What will they do without someone to take charge of them? They'll never make it up Unicorn Mountain."

Maria looked at her companions. Carlos was right of course, they did all need looking after. And he sounded so sure about their plan.

"I guess you're right, but please don't be long. I miss you when you're not around."

"Maria," he answered with a twinkle in his eye, "I'll

be there. I promised didn't I?!"

Maria smiled bravely but rolled her eyes through force of habit. It wasn't that she thought Carlos meant to break his promises, it was more the fact that she was used to him breaking them. And this time, she was really scared that he might not re-appear. This whole cross dimensional travel business wasn't proving to be the easiest thing she had ever done.

Carlos gave Maria a kiss on the cheek before closing the phone box door. Terrence typed in the number that Carlos read to him and the phone box span away in a cloud of green smoke.

"Just the two of us again," said Carlos jovially to Éclair. "Let's go and find your parents."

CHAPTER 24

The phone box settled down on the grass to the over enthusiastic squealing of a pink hyena mixed with the travel sick groans of Steve the tortoise.

"That was terrible," he moaned in his dull and dreary tone. "Let me out, I need some air."

Demonstrating some remarkable teamwork skills, Gladys the galah opened the door using her wood snakes as fully functional arms. Sparkles bounded away with an excited squeal, as the others piled out of the phone box. Maria wasn't quite sure how they had all fit in the first place. Gladys and Sparkles had sat on top of Steve's hard shell which had helped, but it would have been even more of a squeeze if Carlos had been there too.

Carlos....

Maria really wished he was with them. Just as quickly as he'd miraculously appeared, he'd gone again.

Maria sat on a nearby wall whilst Steve recovered. The others stayed close. They had landed in a colourful and vibrant town, where it seemed like everyone had somewhere to be, quickly. There were creatures running around in all directions, hundreds of different species, none of which Maria really knew. Some creatures were similar to those she had seen at home of course, but at home she'd never seen a weasel wearing a Hawaiian shirt on a skateboard. It wasn't what she was used to, but it was a city. Maria felt at home in the city. This seemed like just the kind of place that even Maria's odd little troupe could blend into easily.

Almost too easily. Maria was quite worried about the group getting separated in the crowds, so somebody needed to take charge and make sure the group was organised.

It was going to be Maria of course. Sparkles was too crazy, Steve was too slow, Gladys was too mentally disturbed and Terrence was too stupid. Maria was happy though, she felt good about this place.

After a few minutes it looked like Steve was starting to lose the greenish colour from his cheeks, and Maria thought he looked well enough that they could begin to walk. Maria wanted to find Carlos again quickly, so they must find this mystical Unicorn Mountain as soon as they could. It could be the other side of the planet for all she knew! The first thing they had to do was to work out where they were.

They wandered around the pretty streets, with their colourful shops and houses, but quickly found it intimidating. It was such a busy, bustling place that it was making them all quite dizzy, and without knowing where they were going Maria was a bit worried about going much further in case they got lost. She was quite relieved when a lilting friendly voice cut through the crowd noise.

"Confused? Lost? Let me 'elp you all! Where're you from? Where're you going? I can tell you anyfin', only costs five Ochres!"

They all turned around to see a smiling green lizard in top and tails, standing on his hind legs.

Better keep my eye on him, Maria thought straight away. Although they were marginally less reptilian, Maria had come across many of his type in London, wheeling and dealing, trying to pull the wool over your eyes in the chirpiest manner possible. He was likeable, she had to admit. In fact, her very own Carlos had the same mannerisms at times, although he was far more trustworthy. But she couldn't be too choosy, they did need some help.

"Hello!" she replied, "I could do with some help, but I'm afraid we don't have any Ochres. In fact I don't even know what an Ochre is, we're not from round here."

He quickly filled Maria in on many of the ways in which the Kingdom worked. She was fairly sure she could trust him on this, as he needed to teach her if he was to make any money from them. She quickly learned that Ochre was their currency, and was actually a very common jewel that they all used for trading. She knew they would be able to get some eventually, but negotiated that he would have the simple silver necklace she wore as a returnable deposit – if he was helpful of course. He was happy enough with that, and so was she – it was a £2 fake from Camden market.

"Thanks a lot, we do need some help and some directions. We're after a place called Unicorn Mountain. Do you know it? If you can help us with this as well as finding us a place to stay, I'm sure we can help you out with more than the five Ochres once we've had chance to earn them."

"Unicorn Mountain?" repeated the lizard, who was listening to Maria whilst shaking hands with each member of the party and introducing himself as Clive. "You're in luck, it ain't that far away. I can take you there tomorra'."

"Really?! That's amazing! Thank you so much!"

"Yes, that's very helpful," added Terrence. "We'd never find it by ourselves. We've spent the last few days escaping from an evil scientist in another dimension, now we're lost and we have to get to Unicorn Mountain to meet the only other person we know here. Thank you!"

Although it was a nice sentiment, and possibly the longest number of coherent words Maria had ever heard her brother string together, she saw the instant sparkle in Clive's eyes and wished Terrence had kept quiet. Clive had probably just thought they were lost tourists, who were easy enough to rip-off. But now he knew how much he was needed, he would surely become far more expensive. Maria had a feeling that getting information out of him would now be just that little bit more difficult. Still, they were one step closer to having an actual bed to sleep on for the first time in many nights.

* * *

Having followed Clive through the town for what seemed like an age, they finally stopped in front of a giant pineapple shaped building and one that looked like a Christmas present, all wrapped and ribboned.

"'Ere we are," said Clive, "at my 'umble abode. You can stay with me t'night, and tomorra' I'll tek you up to Unicorn Mountain. But after that you'll either need t' find somewhere else to stay or 'elp me run my business."

"Your business? What's your business?" asked Gladys.

"None o' yours," said Clive, "unless you agree t' work for me. You'll 'ave to sign a waiver and be sworn t' secrecy though."

"Typical," said Steve glumly. "The only person we find to help us is a gangster. We escape from an evil scientist and now we're either gonna get murdered or get imprisoned in an illegal drugs racket. I wish we hadn't bothered escaping from Dr Funk."

As much as Maria wanted to laugh at Steve's dreary outlook on life, she couldn't help but fear his version of the truth slightly. Everything she knew about people indicated to her that Clive was nothing but a wheeler and dealer who didn't want people to know exactly what he was doing. There were plenty of his type in London and she was well used to them. It was a little different here though. They were in a new place and didn't know the dangers or punishments associated with whatever crimes he might be committing, so they had to be careful not to get involved.

"Oh Steve, you are funny," she laughed as she saw the expression of hurt on Clive's face. "Clive, we're very grateful you're helping us and looking after us tonight. Once we've found Carlos we'll know a bit more about what we're planning on doing. Shall we go inside and you can tell us more about the Kingdom of Happiness and All Things Warm and Fluffy?"

"Sounds like a plan, me darlin'," chuckled Clive

heartily. "Folla' me."

Despite their reservations about Clive, the group of friends were very keen to go and rest in comfort. Both the pineapple and present shaped buildings looked extremely posh, and whatever Clive did for a living they were willing to forgive for one night.

They walked straight down the alley between the two buildings and followed him up some steps into his little bedsit.

"It'll be a bit tight," Clive explained as Sparkles shut the front door, just managing to squeeze inside with the rest of them. "But I'm sure we'll be fine."

"I will be," said Steve, and he retracted into his shell out of the way.

"I'll sleep on his shell," said Gladys and clambered on.

Two minutes later Steve popped his head out. "Your scratching claws are keeping me awake. Keep the noise down."

That was the last anyone heard from Steve all night.

CHAPTER 25

Early the next morning, Maria awoke to the sound of Sparkles screeching and bouncing around Clive's bedsit.

"He's got a gun! He's got a gun!" he screamed.

Maria peered out of the back window and could see Clive in his workshop, cleaning a small pistol with a rag. *"How could I have misjudged him so badly?"* she thought. He couldn't be the chirpy and harmless wheeler and dealer she had expected, anyone who needed a gun for protection was likely to be mixed up in something really sinister.

It didn't take much encouragement to rouse Steve and Gladys. Maria fumbled with the lock on the front door and they rushed down the steps into the alleyway. Walking back past the pineapple and present-shaped buildings, they retraced their steps from the night before. Maria had learned from Clive that the buses to Unicorn Mountain stopped on the same road as where they had met him.

Maria had a good memory and sense of direction, so even through the busy streets they found their way back to the phone box easily. As they rounded another corner, Maria recognised a blue tower curling gracefully into the sky.

"This is the road we landed on!" she said triumphantly, pleased that they hadn't got lost on the way. Spotting a number of brightly coloured shelters nearby, they stood, patiently waiting for the bus to Unicorn Mountain. They had been standing there for a good ten minutes, and Gladys was starting to get a little stressed. It didn't help when she spotted a familiar figure approaching.

"He's here! Clive's coming to kill us!" squawked Gladys all in a panic, her wood snakes hissing around her in anger. Sure enough, Maria could see Clive running around the corner, with a gun in one hand and a tea towel in the other.

"Come back!" he shouted. "Come back! Where're you goin'?!"

This was a conversation they had no intention of having, so the friends pushed their way through the crowds. There was only one place they could possibly go to get away - the phone box.

"Nine nine nine!" shouted Sparkles. "Nine nine nine!!" 999 was the number for Dr Funk's emergency services in $E=mc^2$ and Sparkles assumed it would be the same everywhere.

Thinking it as good an idea as any, the ragtag of creatures climbed back into the phone box and Terrence dialled.

The call was answered within seconds.

"Hello... Emergency services! Which service do you require?"

"Police! Police!" Terrence shouted. "Quickly!"

"Calm down dear," said the voice. "You'll be there in a second."

The phone box started to spin and The Kingdom of All Things Warm and Fluffy flashed out of view.

They all gave out a collective sigh of relief.

"Why does this always happen to us?" asked Steve glumly. "It's quite unfair."

Maria had a sudden sinking feeling. They were changing dimension again. "How are we going to find Carlos now?!" she cried. "Does anyone remember the number to get back to the Kingdom of Happiness and All Things Warm and Fluffy?"

Terrence shook his head glumly.

"Elephants never forget," said Steve solemnly. "But unfortunately, none of us contain any elephant parts."

Before Maria could thank Steve for his helpful insight, the phone box came to a standstill.

Maria looked outside in amazement.

"This isn't a police station!" cried Terrence.

They had arrived in the hugest shopping store in the entire universe. Excitedly, Maria got out of the phone box and stood next to a massive fountain, which was the centrepiece for each of the one hundred and sixty seven storeys. Looking around her she could see racks of clothes stretching into the distance, sparkling shoes everywhere, and handbags galore.

A funny looking man wearing platform heels and a gravity defying spherical Mohican hairstyle was tottering towards them.

"Well hello darlings!" he greeted enthusiastically. "Welcome to Unicorn Hill, home of the Fashion Police."

The others muttered greetings, a little taken aback by the super confident fashionista. He was far from the policeman they had envisaged.

"Oh dear," he said, looking Sparkles up and down. "Springs with pink hyena? That's sooo last season..."

Sparkles slumped despondently on his springs. It wasn't his fault Dr Funk was behind the times.

The man glanced around the group, a derisory look on his face.

"I see we're going to have our work cut out with all of you," he said. "But never fear, you've come to the right place. Follow me!"

The bemused group began to follow him towards a set of glass elevators.

"Did you say we were at Unicorn Hill?" asked Maria quietly. "Is that the same thing as Unicorn Mountain?"

"Yes and no!" answered the man, throwing his arms around with unnecessary theatricals. "You have arrived at Unicorn Hill, the biggest and greatest shopping experience in the universe! Unicorn Hill is located right next to Unicorn Mountain, as close as you could possibly be without being on it."

"We're next to it? That's great!" enthused Maria. "See, we need to climb Unicorn Mountain so that we can meet my boyfriend at the top."

"Oh, I see," said the man sneering at the modest skirt Maria was wearing. "So you want slutty but practical then? We can do that. It's warm out there. Heavy duty fishnets with convertible walking heels should sort you out. Maybe a..."

"No!" Maria interrupted. "I like my clothes! I was just wondering how we could get up there as quickly as possible!"

"You like your clothes?" said the man, an expression of surprise and disdain etched across his face. "I'm sorry, but I am the great Lemon Drizzle, and I won't let anybody walk the globe dressed like that! I will tell you all about the Unicorn Mountain but not until we have made you look faborific!"

They had now reached the lifts and it was clear they were all going to get a makeover whether they liked it or not. Maria was at least pleased that they had got to Unicorn Mountain without too many problems.

Each member of the group was taken into a different lift by one of Lemon Drizzle's many colleagues and whisked off to various parts of the store. Maria got the pleasure of the boss's company.

Matty Millard

CHAPTER 26

"They've said you can help," said Éclair after a heated debate with a group of jelly babies. Whilst flying around searching for Éclair's parents, Carlos and Éclair had stumbled across some of her jelly baby friends who were trying to rebuild the Jelly Village after the merging of dimensions had caused many of the houses to turn into rock. This wasn't acceptable to the jelly babies, they themselves ate rocks and wanted their houses to be made from gingerbread, chocolate and biscuits, not food.

After a little while, the initial commotion caused by Carlos's attempts to help had stopped. The jelly babies still didn't want him anywhere near their village, but he could lift up and place huge chunks of gingerbread on the roof a lot more easily than the jelly babies. It would save them weeks of work. Carlos was quite glad he had a chance to do something to help them, to make amends for his misdemeanours.

Whilst Carlos was busying himself, Éclair was chatting away to some of her friends. Unfortunately, none of them had seen her parents anywhere. Carlos and Éclair had flown around for the whole day, and had seen nothing either. They had been to all sides of the land, and Carlos had even endured a frightening few hours of flying around in an arnmod fashion over the sea. Carlos was petrified of a splash-landing, but Éclair explained to him that the exploration was necessary "just in case they are flying around looking for me." They both knew with growing certainty that they wouldn't find them, even if neither wanted to say it.

After helping out at the Jelly Village, Éclair decided she wanted just one last fly around before the day was up. Carlos agreed, and they decided to return to where they began their search. As they flew back over Dr Funk's lair they could see him outside, marshalling some of his remaining troops. Well, less marshalling and more bawling at.

"You will find those wretched creatures, they've ruined everything!"

His troops stared at him, not daring to even blink. He was crazy even when he was normal, but this definitely wasn't the time to be singled out for any reason.

"The most important one is that Gladys – I need her back! She is my ultimate weapon! And now that they've stolen the Torch of Darkness, I cannot make another being as evil as her."

Despairing, head in his hands, he muttered to himself. "It took me years to make that torch, I'm not sure I could do it again..."

Pulling himself together, he continued to his troops. "Listen to this carefully. It is vitally important that you do not smear any apricot jam on Gladys – that will trigger the destruction sequence, and that cannot happen until she is in Sandwich. If you find Carlos, I want him alive. He is their ringleader and he has hidden them somewhere clever, I can feel it. The rest of them, do whatever is necessary."

It was at this very moment that the greasy teenager's huge, massive, throbbing pimple burst.

Carlos and Éclair got covered in custard. Éclair started to cry.

CHAPTER 27

The teary-eyed Éclair blew her nose, and drowned a nearby field in squirty cream.

"Do you think we'll ever find them again?" she asked Carlos of her parents.

"I'm sure we'll find them somewhere in another dimension," replied Carlos, placing a comforting arm around the giant cake dragon's leg. "That book told me about it, remember? I know it's all very confusing us having changed dimensions and everything, but they'll be absolutely fine in whatever dimension they have been moved to."

Carlos wasn't entirely sure about this, but he'd learned over the last few days that little in the universe made sense, so it was definitely possible. Parallel dimensions **were** squiggly.

"Where do you think they are?" asked Éclair.

"I don't know," admitted Carlos. "They are probably still in Pink River, but I guess they could be in whatever dimension those Venus fly-traps came from. Remember them?!"

Éclair giggled as she pictured them snogging next to Dr Funk.

"Wherever they are, they'll be fine," assured Carlos. "We'll go and find them after we've found Maria and the others. Is that ok?"

Reluctantly, the cake dragon agreed to give up searching the new merged dimension they were in (E-numbers = Minty Candy Canes) and travel to the Kingdom of Happiness and All Things Warm and Fluffy to find Carlos's friends. It would be easier to find them if they had a whole group of people looking for them after all.

That meant that it was finally time to try out this contraption that Carlos had inherited off Dr Oliver[2]. It dawned on Carlos that they had never tried it before! If it didn't actually work they were stuck here with the evil Dr Funk, forever! He decided not to share his fears with the already emotionally fragile Éclair.

"This is called The WorldChanger," he announced, pulling the device out of his satchel.

Nervously, he unfolded The WorldChanger, fastened one bulldog clip to his shirt and another to one of Éclair's sponge scales. Éclair swore it didn't hurt, but Carlos could tell she was just trying to appear brave. *She's doing a very good job of it to be honest,* he thought. Losing your parents at the tender age of eight was one thing, travelling to an unknown dimension with a relative stranger to escape a mad scientist who wanted to blow up a whole planet was another.

"To The Kingdom of Happiness!!" Carlos shouted triumphantly as he finished typing in the number, and the two friends were engulfed by green smoke. As it got thicker, he heard Éclair laugh.

"Carlos, why are you so scared?!" she giggled.

"I'm not!" he insisted. "I've done this loads of times!" This was sort of true, if accidental dimension changes counted towards the total.

"So why are you holding onto my leg?" she asked as the pair became weightless and the candy-floss plains were whisked out of sight.

"I'm not!" replied Carlos.

Spluttering[21], Éclair looked around her. They were definitely in a brand new world. In front of her was a giant unicorn, standing next to her was Carlos, and holding onto her leg as if his life depended on it was a stunned Dr Funk.

"Look!" Carlos gasped in awe. "Unicorn Mountain!"

The unicorn, although it was at least two hundred times bigger than the cake dragon, took one look at Éclair and galloped away, squealing with fright.

---

21   Cake dragons are highly allergic to green smoke. Never take one on a weekend break to Amsterdam.

CHAPTER 28

Maria was putting on a sparkling blue stoned necklace when the world began to shake violently. She screamed, threw herself to the floor and wrapped her arms around her head for protection as clothes fell from the shelves all around.

"EARTHQUAKE!" she screamed.

"No it's not! Don't worry dear!" calmed Lemon Drizzle, patting Maria's hair to soothe her. "This happens all the time, it's just the unicorn running around."

"The unicorn?" asked Maria incredulously. "You have unicorns here?"

"Yes, Unicorn Mountain is one. Don't you know anything about it?"

"No, nothing."

"Really? Well darling, I must fill you in hadn't I? How long have we got?" He looked at his wrist where a watch might have been, but his arms were covered by long frilly lace gloves. He sighed. "Oh, one of these days I'll wear something functional you know. And then I know

I'll be too old!" He tittered away to himself for a while before continuing. "Anyway, Unicorn Mountain."

Maria sat quietly, trying to concentrate on Lemon's story whilst glancing nervously around for objects that might fall on her.

"Once upon a time, he was just a small unicorn called Reginald, running carefree throughout the lands. Everyone liked him, he was a lovely kid. On his eighteenth birthday, he officially became an adult unicorn called Reginald. Now unicorns, as nature will have it, stop growing on their eighteenth birthday but this wasn't the case with our Reginald. No, Reginald carried on growing at the same rate as his teen years, and he is still growing to this day. Reginald, or Unicorn Mountain as he is more commonly known, is now almost four hundred thousand years old. Unicorns are not meant to be immortal, but for some reason Reginald has never died of old age – despite the fact that he is clearly very old. No, Reginald appears to have escaped all of nature's usual laws, and has become the unicorn that we see today."

Maria opened her mouth as if to speak, but Lemon Drizzle silenced her with the theatrical wave of a seasoned storyteller.

"How did Reginald become a mountain I hear you ask? Well, it's quite simple really. On his one hundred thousandth birthday, he announced to the world that he had been walking around doing the job of a grown unicorn for far too long and without even a single day's paid holiday. So he handed in his notice at the dry cleaners he worked in, lay down, and slept for fifty thousand years. During that time many hikers got lost and accidentally walked up him. After a while he became part of the coastal path and was drawn onto the map.

Eventually though, he woke up as he needed to go to the bathroom. Happy to hear that he had provided a great deal of enjoyment to people around the world, Reginald agreed to remain a public right of way to hikers, albeit one that could run around. Nowadays you have to be flexible in location if you want to go walking on Unicorn Mountain. Reginald, of course, also wanted some control over the people who wandered around his body. You wouldn't just want any Tom, Dick or Harry hopping on your back would you?"

Maria shook her head at the prompt.

"So nowadays you must earn the right to climb Unicorn Mountain. He loves a good song, but if you can't sing a decent story will suffice. Otherwise you must dazzle him with your charming personality! The latter is always the riskiest approach, but I'm sure you won't have any worries there, my darling." Lemon Drizzle flashed a lecherous smile at Maria.

"So how do we get onto Unicorn Mountain, erm... sorry, Reginald? If he's always running around that is?" Maria asked. "I'm supposed to be meeting my boyfriend at the top so we need to hike up there."

"You did say so already," replied Lemon testily. Twice he had reacted badly to Maria's mention of a boyfriend, but given his overly flirtatious manner Maria thought it prudent that she should remind him.

"Well that **is** who I'm meeting," said Maria impatiently. Boys who couldn't take a hint frustrated her. If she had flirted with Lemon Drizzle she could understand it, but she'd made it completely obvious that she had a boyfriend.

Lemon shrugged dismissively. "Oh it's very difficult,

climbing Unicorn Mountain," he explained, taking the opportunity to try to put Maria off finding Carlos. "You have to stun the unicorn with a song at one of his pre-defined boarding points. But before that you'll need to fight your way through the jungle."

"Through the jungle? But he's only there!" Maria pointed at the unicorn through the shop windows.

"Well in a way, I suppose you're right. There must only be a few metres between Unicorn Hill and Unicorn Mountain. But that short distance is entirely comprised of the inter-dimensional membrane. We're extremely lucky to be able to see Reginald from outside his home dimension."

Of course, thought Maria, *we used the phone box again didn't we?*

She asked the question which had worried her when the used the phone box to get to Unicorn Hill. "We are going to be able to get back to the same dimension aren't we? I don't remember the number!"

"Don't worry darling!" re-assured Lemon. "We're the emergency services, we can send you right back there!" No sooner had he said this he recoiled in horror. *How stupid are you?! I could have kept her here after all! All it would have taken was a little white lie..."*

Annoyed with himself but signalling extravagantly that he was happy with Maria's new outfit, Lemon strutted out of the room with the air and poise of an experienced diva. She followed him into the lift and they wound their way back downwards towards the entrance. She struggled not to laugh at the decidedly unimpressed looking Steve, who was sitting in the foyer wearing a straw hat with a yellow ribbon tied around his shell.

"Oh Steve!" said Maria. "You look adorable! Like a pretty little Easter present."

"This is worse than that watermelon I used to wear," said Steve truthfully.

Gladys walked in, dressed as normal[22].

Lemon Drizzle's assistants walked a few yards behind her, clearly scared of something.

"Ha! Look at you two!" she squawked. "Steve, you look adorable!"

"Adorable....." he repeated with hatred mixed into every syllable. "Really? Abhorrable maybe…"

"Oh Steve," said Maria, adjusting his hat. "That's not even a word. And anyway you look lovely!"

"I hate to disagree," he said. "Anyway Gladys, how did you avoid this?"

"Well it seems that these snakes I've inherited do exactly what I want them to. Those fashion fascists are going to be tending to their bites for weeks!" Gladys looked rather pleased with her new arms.

Just as they were settling down, along came Sparkles. Everyone looked up in amazement.

A pink hyena, dressed in a snazzy white suit, with a pink top hat and giant pink platform heels marched, not bounced, confidently into the room.

"Hey there," he said in a deep and velvety voice. "Loving this new look. Steve, that's one hell of a ribbon. Maria, you look delightful. Carlos is a lucky man."

The others were gob-smacked.

---

22   As in, she wasn't dressed. Gladys was a galah. Galahs wear feathers.

Matty Millard

CHAPTER 29

Maria, Steve, Gladys and the new sophisticated and confident Sparkles crammed into the phone box ready to return to the Kingdom of Happiness and All Things Warm and Fluffy. Maria politely thanked Lemon Drizzle for their outfits, the information on Unicorn Mountain and the map he had given her so that they could find their way to one of Reginald's boarding stops. Resisting the offer of a goodbye kiss[23], and then fighting off a goodbye hug[24], she closed the phone box door and typed in the number Lemon had given her.

The familiar green smoke rose and they reappeared in the Kingdom of Happiness and All Things Warm and Fluffy. Fortunately they weren't in the middle of the town they had left when Terrence dialled "999," it seemed that Lemon had sent them to the rainforest he had told her about, near to Unicorn Mountain.

A sudden realisation hit Maria. *Terrence had dialled 999!*

---

23   Snog
24   Grope

"Steve… where's Terrence?"

Terrence had been forgotten in the excitement! She'd been far too busy fussing over Steve, and Sparkles's new look had completely thrown her.

"Hmmm… good question," Steve replied. "He's not here."

"I can see that," said Maria. "We must have left him at Unicorn Hill."

"True. He's lucky though. He's not wearing a stupid ribbon."

"How do you know?" asked Sparkles. "He might be. He might have two. Maria, don't worry, we'll just go back and get him. No problem."

Still, Maria felt an unquenchable guilt for leaving her brother in Lemon Drizzle's shopping centre. It was easily done though, he was very quiet and you often just assumed he was there, somewhere in the background. This wasn't the first time he had got lost in a shopping centre either. She remembered when they were little and their parents had lost Terrence in Matalan only to find that he had got his head stuck in a coat-hanger and was strung up on a rack of Levi Strauss jeans.

Needless to say, she rang "999" so that they could return to Unicorn Hill and fetch Terrence.

"Hello… Emergency services! Which service do you require?" said the voice down the phone.

"Fashion Police please," replied Maria politely.

"Again?" asked the operator. "But you've only just returned from there! I'm afraid that this is an emergency service and as such you are unable to return within three months. After thirty seconds, you can hardly be in an emergency situation again. Do you think we are made of money?"

"No! No of course not!" replied Maria hurriedly. "I don't want any more clothes, we've left my brother!"

"Ahh, I see," replied the operator. "A likely story. Some people will try anything to get more new clothes."

"No! It's true! Honestly!"

"Whatever. Brian, we've got another crazy female on the line claiming they've lost someone in Unicorn Hill. Do you want to come and deal with her?"

A new voice entered the conversation. It was deep and gruff, and didn't sound like the most patient voice in the world.

"Right," Brian began. "We get crazy women like you on the phone all the time. Why don't you just try honesty? If you want more clothes, then just ask. Who knows, it might even work."

Maria decided to change tack.

"Ok, you've got me. We landed in a muddy field, I slipped over and I'm absolutely covered. I can't go around looking like this!"

"See," answered Brian. "That wasn't so difficult was it? If you'd just said that in the first place, you'd have saved us a whole load of pointless conversation."

"You're going to send us back?!" gushed Maria, relief flowing through her body. "Thank you so much!"

"No," said Brian. "U......nlucky."

He hung up.

Flushed with anger, Maria tried again but the number wouldn't even ring out.

Maria turned to the others, worry etched on her face. "We can't go back! What are we going to do?"

"I wouldn't worry," said Sparkles, whose whole

personality had transformed, not just his outfit. He was no longer the hysterical giggling bouncing mess that had irritated the others with regularity, a well-spoken and considered Sparkles had now taken over. Of course, the new Sparkles would reason that he didn't say anything different, he had merely acquired a mentality which allowed him to express himself better. "Lemon Drizzle will find him and send him back. Terrence knows where we are going, he'll meet us there."

"This is Terrence, Sparkles," said Maria, forcing back a tear. "He'll never find Unicorn Mountain. And if he does, he's not really a born entertainer. I've seen him clear pubs in seconds on the karaoke. I'm not sure that Reginald will let him on if he has to dazzle him with intelligent and stimulating conversation."

"Good point," said Steve in his usual dreary voice. "Terrence is quite stupid."

"And his eyes are too close together!" squawked Gladys, oblivious to the irony of a galah who had living wooden snakes instead of wings commenting on someone's appearance.

"He's not stupid!" shouted Maria, defensive of Terrence even though she had said pretty much the same thing. She was allowed to insult him, he was her brother.

"He'll be fine, Maria," said Sparkles. "From what I've seen of him so far I think he'll probably just wait for us to return to the phone box with Carlos."

Grateful for Sparkles's unflappable rationality[25], Maria felt a bit better. He was probably right. Terrence was

---

25 Nowadays, Sparkles was as unflappable as Gladys had always been, and far more rational.

usually too scared to do stuff by himself, so he would wait for them by the phone box when Lemon Drizzle sends him back. What was she worried about? They can go and find Carlos, then return to fetch Terrence later.

They'd better get a move on though, so they could get back as soon as possible. She didn't want Terrence to think they had completely forgotten about him.

Meanwhile, back in Unicorn Hill, Lemon Drizzle was rubbing his hands. *Maria's forgotten her brother!* He laughed, almost as if he'd meant it to happen. *She'll be so grateful when I return him to her, that stupid boyfriend of hers won't stand a chance next to me!*

Terrence was still struggling to get free of the coathanger Lemon had forced over his head.

CHAPTER 30

"What are you doing here?" asked Carlos accusingly. "We don't want you! Stop following us!"

"Not until I have what I came for!" shouted the evil Dr Funk hysterically.

"So what **have** you come for? Your Ultimate Weapon can't hurt Sandwich from here!"

Dr Funk looked taken aback. "H... how do you know about that?" he asked.

"Never you mind. All I know is that we will find Gladys before you ever can, and we will take her far away from here. You will never see her again!"

Carlos could see the irritation growing on Dr Funk's face.

"You think so? Well if I follow you I might just change that hadn't I? And that way I get to blow you all up!"

Carlos was getting really tired of Dr Funk. He was evil, annoying and strangely unintelligent for a scientific genius.

"Step on him, Éclair! Squash him!" shouted Carlos,

desperate to see the end of this crazy man who had done so much to hurt his friends.

Éclair lifted her foot up high above his head. Dr Funk froze, cowering in her giant shadow.

Éclair put her foot down.

"I can't do it Carlos," she apologised, shaking her head. "I don't think I could ever kill someone, no matter how horrible they are."

Carlos wasn't angry with Éclair, in fact he was annoyed with himself for asking such a thing of her. He wasn't sure if he would have been able to do it either. Besides, how can you possibly get angry with a dragon made of cake?

Dr Funk started jumping around, whooping and taunting Éclair. "Ha! You're pathetic! You'll never stop me!"

Éclair pinned Dr Funk to the floor with a single breath of squirty cream. She lifted Carlos onto her back and they flew off into the sky, leaving the evil Dr Funk all by himself. They both hoped that this would be the last time they ever saw him.

CHAPTER 31

Maria roused the troops ready for their journey to Unicorn Mountain. Lemon Drizzle had given her plenty of information about it. It wasn't that far, they just had to go directly through the dark and foreboding rainforest in front of them.

"I thought this place was supposed to be Warm and Fluffy," groaned Steve.

He had a point. The rainforest towered in front of them, a mass of tangled vines and gnarled old tree trunks. The path they had to take was lost to view almost immediately as it wound into the darkness. Screeching of monkeys and relentless clicking of insects filled them with dread as to what might be in there. A giant rain-cloud hovering above it completed the picture.

"The rain's not a problem," Maria told herself. *"It's a **rain**forest. It's part of the experience."*

She secretly wished it wasn't raining though, or that she had at least got her lucky polka-dot umbrella with her.

There was probably only a couple of hours walk in

front of them, so Maria thought they should go and get it over with. It was a big plus that Sparkles had calmed down so much. Maria wouldn't have fancied trying to take the old Sparkles through such an intimidating environment. Rainforests are always full of weird and dangerous things, and Maria didn't really want to disturb whatever might be lurking in the depths.

On entering the rainforest Maria noticed straight away that it was visibly darker. The trees, giant ferns and creeping vines were all so densely packed that she could only see a few yards in each direction. The light filtered through in what seemed like individual rays. Shadows jumped, leaves rustled, and water dripped. Maria flinched at the every insect click or bird whistle, expecting every noise to reveal some hidden danger.

Steve was right. I'm not Happy, Warm or Fluffy at all.

Sparkles strutted around, forging the way ahead with Maria but regularly dropping back to encourage the slower paced Steve who was doing his best to keep up. Maria was usually quite good at making sure everyone in the party was ok, but the rainforest had made her so jumpy that she was unusually quiet, her sole focus was on following the path and getting out of there. She set a fast pace, and her progress was good. But she jumped a mile when she heard a loud shriek and a squawk from behind her.

She turned, but could see nothing. "Gladys?!" she shouted. "GLADYS!"

Sparkles put his hand on her shoulder and signalled for her to be quiet. She was, and looked to him for further instructions. As quickly and stealthily as they could, they made their way back along the path until they heard a deep and depressed "Oh... No."

"Steve!" she whispered urgently, glancing at Sparkles who remained calm.

Sparkles forged ahead, to see what was happening. Unfortunately, stealth in a pair of pink platform shoes was fairly difficult, and Maria winced as a twig snapped with a huge *"CRACK"*. She spotted something moving through the trees in front of him as Sparkles turned and ran.

They had probably run for about 200 metres before their pursuers caught up. Maria felt something heavy land on her back, and she fell face first into the wet undergrowth. Sparkles fell alongside her with a refined shriek.

She looked towards him, only to see lots of spear-waving green cavemen with red unicorn horns on their foreheads running around them. "Not again," she groaned, as she was dragged along the floor towards a mossy cave.

Matty Millard

CHAPTER 32

Maria was fed up of being kidnapped. She'd always kept herself to herself and as such had never been in any real trouble back in London. Now that she'd inadvertently left home, she had been kidnapped twice in quick succession! Although this irritated her immensely, she did feel like she was getting better at being kidnapped with practise. This experience was a lot better than being imprisoned in a dark dank cell by Dr Funk. She was being treated really well!

Maria was sitting on a comfortable green sofa next to Gladys, eating cucumber sandwiches cut into triangles and supping tea off the best bone china. It was all quite civilised. The little green cavemen hadn't said much yet, but one of them was sitting, smiling politely, on a slightly higher and more grand-looking green sofa in front of them. The horn on his forehead had changed to white, which unbeknown to Maria at this point, symbolised his mood of tranquillity.

Maria had noticed that he wore a necklace made of threaded bones around his neck. As none of the others had worn one, she assumed that this set him aside as the leader.

Maria finished her tea and set her cup down carefully on the saucer.

"Would you like some more?" asked the little green caveman.

"No thanks," she replied politely. "I'm all full up thank you."

Maria believed that even when kidnapped one should always display good manners at a tea party.

The little green caveman looked at her and smiled, without saying a further word. Maria found herself staring at the horn on his forehead. It was still pure white, just like that of a unicorn.

"So..." she coughed nervously, trying not to stare. "Have we been kidnapped? It's quite hard to tell, what with the tea and sandwiches and everything."

"Kidnapped?! Noooo. Whatever gave you that idea?" asked the little green man, his horn flashing to a light orange.

"Well, being chased and then dived on and then forcibly dragged to your village," answered Maria as calmly as she could.

"Oh, that!" laughed the little green man, his horn turning straight back to white. "Sorry about that. We kind of have to do that nowadays. It's very difficult to get party guests otherwise. They all run away as soon as they see us, just like **he** did," he accused, pointing at Sparkles.

Sparkles looked truly sorry as he replied. "Yes, I did run away and I apologise for my behaviour. But you did look quite frightening, what with waving your clubs around and your spiky horns. And you had already

140

kidnapped Steve and Gladys."

"No we hadn't!"

"Hadn't you?"

"No!"

"But…"

"It's true," interjected Steve.

"So… what was all the shouting about?"

"I… err … fell in a hole," said Steve.

"You fell in a hole?"

"Yes. We were walking so quickly," said Steve, who must have reached a mind boggling half a mile per hour maximum ambling speed through the rainforest. "It made me all dizzy, and I tripped and fell in a ditch. Gladys tried to catch me with her wood snake arms, but they just bit me and it was all a bit uncomfortable really. Then the cavemen came and pulled me out. They were very nice actually."

"Oh. Right. So I guess you are a race of serial tea party hosts then," said Sparkles.

"We are."

"Then I have to admit that I misjudged you and find you very nice and hospitable. I hope you can accept my most sincere apologies."

"We do, and thank you."

"As a bright pink hyena I guess I should be more sensitive when it comes to judging people on first impressions," said Sparkles eloquently.

As well as being more than slightly disbelieving of the surreal situation they found themselves in, Maria was both relieved and amazed. Sparkles had changed completely. He was smooth talking, polite and made a lot of sense. Maybe he could even part-fill the gap that

Carlos had temporarily left and help her look after the other members of the group.

"I'm Maria," she ventured, sensing that the cavemen were actually friendly. She then introduced the rest of her party.

"Nice to meet you all. I'm High Lord Guaranchinga of the East-Western Base Foothill Tribe of Unimen. But you can call me Pete."

"Hi Pete," the travellers chorused happily. Except for Steve of course who grunted grumpily. He was still embarrassed about falling in a hole, and had known he had been completely helpless, lying on his back with his legs waving in the air. But even worse, he still hadn't got over the ribbon he was wearing and nobody would help him take it off. His clumpy feet weren't designed for dressing and undressing.

"So what were you doing wandering around the rainforest?" asked Pete.

"We're actually looking to climb Unicorn Mountain, we're supposed to be meeting my boyfriend at the top," answered Maria. "We were told this was the best way."

"Unicorn Mountain? Why didn't you say so sooner?!" cried Pete. "Reginald will be here anytime now, we've got to move fast!"

Within minutes Pete was leading the group out of the Unimen Village and back into the wilds of the rainforest.

"Come on! Come on!" he cajoled.

Pete was not impressed by Steve's fastest ambling speed. "We'll never get there on time," he lamented. "We should have left hours ago..."

"I'm sorry," said Steve sadly, but he didn't mean it. He was in a bad mood today. Not only was he wearing a straw hat and a yellow ribbon, but he had been forced to sit through a typically posh tea party. It went against all his beliefs, as tortoises have a big problem with triangular sandwiches. Maria had warned him not to make an issue of it.

"But they're unnatural!" he moaned. "If God had meant us to eat triangular sandwiches, he would have invented at least one triangular shaped loaf of bread[26]."

By nodding in placatory agreement with Steve's logic, Maria managed to prevent him from outright complaining, but he had carried on chuntering away to himself for the whole tea party.

Eventually they reached the Unicorn Mountain boarding stop which was marked by a giant green cone. Next to the cone was a long line of people. I say people; there were dwarves, Unimen, viper-squirrels, badger-lords, mermaids, treefolk, and kangaroo-dragon-fish[27] amongst many more.

"There are a lot of people waiting," said Maria. "So we can't have missed him!"

But Pete looked puzzled. "Something doesn't look

---

26 By God, Steve meant the Irreverent God of the Shelled Creatures, Slouch, who was worshipped for his legendary performance in a running race against a prehistoric rabbit.

27 Kangaroo-dragon-fish are an interesting race. They are well known in the Kingdom of Happiness and All Things Warm and Fluffy for being very susceptible to schizophrenia. If you ever get invited to a kangaroo-dragon-fish's house for tea, don't turn up until you know its cooked. Preparation of their world famous accidental seaweed soup pancake is usually quite traumatic. The mixing together of seaweed, tadpoles, garlic and freshwater usually goes well. It's when the dragon takes over to heat the thing that it all goes wrong, and the kangaroo has to jump all over it to put the fire out.

right to me. Just give me a minute." He went over to speak to some of those who were waiting.

After a while he came back, his horn glowing red to signal his worry.

"It's not good news, Reginald hasn't been past for two whole days. I wonder where he could have got to." Pete looked around, deep in thought. "Shall we walk to the edge of the rainforest and have a look? It's not far, and we'll be able to see him from anywhere once we're out of the trees."

Everyone nodded in agreement. They were all keen to get out of the eerie rainforest, so they followed Pete along the overgrown path towards daylight.

It didn't take too long, even at Steve's excruciatingly slow pace, to reach the spot that Pete was aiming for.

"Thank goodness for that!" exclaimed Maria when they got outside into the daylight. "I was starting to get really creeped out in there."

"Really?" said Pete. "Well there's no reason to, everything is quite friendly here. We are the Kingdom of Happiness and all Things Warm and Fluffy after all. Come here, let me prove it to you."

Reluctantly, Maria followed him back to the edge of the rainforest.

"You see these trees that you think are so spooky? Touch one. Go on, that one there."

A little bemused, Maria touched the tree. It was soft! In fact, it felt quite spongy.

"Hug it!" instructed Pete.

Maria looked at him, a quizzical look on her face.

"Go on," he encouraged, "don't be scared."

Not feeling scared, but feeling very silly, Maria put both arms around the tree. Feeling something on her back, she screamed and jumped backwards! Whatever it was had disappeared.

"Come on Maria," laughed Pete. "It's completely safe, believe me. Give it a proper hug."

Apprehensive and confused, Maria did. She had grown to trust Pete the Uniman very quickly. Again, she felt a firm sensation on her back but this time she wasn't startled. A few seconds later she realised what it was.

"The tree is hugging me back!" Maria shouted, a big grin on her face.

Pete laughed and confirmed that she was right. The others followed her over and they all found a tree. It was such a strange concept that they all wanted to know what it was about.

So the tree-hugging began, and they all laughed and felt a lot better about the Kingdom of Happiness and All Things Warm and Fluffy. Except, of course, for Steve.

"I can't feel anything," he moaned. "I think my shell is too thick for hugging."

He looked a little depressed, but Gladys was in a very good mood. It was the first time in years that she had been hugged and she felt amazing. Hugging is quite a difficult skill for a galah with no wings, but now she had her wood snake arms it was a different matter. Gladys wandered over and gave the tortoise a big comforting squeeze.

"Better?" she asked.

Steve looked a little embarrassed but confirmed that he was.

"Anyway," said Pete. "I hate to interrupt the love-in, but I can spy a giant Unicorn."

The loved-up comrades all turned around for their first sight of Reginald.

CHAPTER 33

As Carlos lay in the shade of a purple coconut tree, he struggled to relax and clear his mind. The thought that currently occupied him was his sheer amazement at Éclair's bravery, resilience and compassion. She was an eight year old child, albeit a giant dragon, who had lost her parents, all of her friends and ended up in a completely different dimension. She was handling it all so much better than he was - at least he knew that his Maria was here somewhere for support. She must be scared though, somewhere deep inside. Carlos both marvelled and worried about her.

Little did Carlos know that being scared was as far away from Éclair's mind as it could be at the moment.

Whilst Carlos was trying to sleep, Éclair had gone off for a proper exploration of the Kingdom of Happiness and All Things Warm and Fluffy. She loved it. It was so colourful, vibrant and interesting. It reminded her a little bit of home, except that everything was a bit bigger. She liked that. Of course she had loved her jelly baby friends back in Pink River, but she had found herself squinting quite a lot to work out who was who.

Whilst practising some loop-the-loops and other airborne frolics, she was blissfully unaware that she had a spectator.

Eventually Éclair noticed the fluffy blue dragon sitting on a cloud. He waved, and smiled. Éclair became conscious of her flying again and plummeted, still looping the loop, towards the ground. She landed in a heap, panting for breath.

The watching dragon landed next to her.

"Are you alright?" he asked, genuinely concerned. "I'm sorry if I startled you."

Éclair tried to speak but was partly winded and partly shy.

"Yes. I'm ok," she croaked. "Thanks."

"I'm so glad," continued the blue dragon. "That looked like quite a heavy fall. Can I help you up?"

Éclair gave him her hand and he hauled her back to her feet. She groaned a little with pain.

"I landed on one of my buns," she explained. "I think I've squashed it."

The blue dragon looked a bit embarrassed. He wasn't sure what she meant by buns so changed the conversation.

"Oh, I'm sorry," he continued. "I'm Blueberry. I'm nine years old. Who are you? I've never seen you before."

"I'm Éclair and I'm eight. I'm from Pink River, it's in another dimension."

"Another dimension?! Cool! Can you travel through them like the unicorns?"

"Like unicorns? They can travel dimensions? Awesome! I can't travel them really, but my friend

Carlos has this special invention which transports you to different ones. You just have to type the right number in," explained Éclair. "We've just come from one dimension where we had to rescue Maria from a crazy scientist called Dr Funk! But now he's followed us here, so I covered him in squirty cream and we left him in a field miles away! And now we've gotta go and meet Maria at the top of Unicorn Mountain so that we can all escape before he gets there!"

"Wow! That's so amazing! Do you want to come to my house for tea? I want you to tell me everything about your adventures!"

"Yes please! I can't stay long though, I've gotta take Carlos to Unicorn Mountain after he's had a quick nap. Are there more dragons at your house?"

"Yes!" replied Blueberry, "there are lots more dragons and they're all really friendly! Come on then, follow me!"

Éclair's flight nervousness was forgotten and she followed her new friend excitedly through the skies. It had been a long, long time since she had seen any other dragons.

CHAPTER 35

Éclair followed Blueberry over rocky mountains and vast forests, raging rivers and picturesque meadows. They spiralled upwards, piercing through the fluffy white clouds. The sight on the other side took her breath away.

It was beautiful. On a plateau floating up in the heavens were green plains stretching away into the distance. There were gushing waterfalls, huge glistening lakes, and most importantly, dragons. Everywhere.

They were all different shapes and sizes, and an array of bright colours.

"This is amazing!!" cried Éclair. "I've never seen so many dragons in my life!"

Blueberry gave her a wide smile as a couple of inquisitive dragons bounded over excitedly.

"Blueberry!" a little green fluffy boy dragon cried. "You have a new friend! And she's multi-coloured!"

"Yeah, this is Éclair. She's from a different dimension!"

"Wow!" said the little purple girl dragon next to him. "That's so cool! Are you made of cake?! I wish I was made of cake, it's so beautiful! I'm Lavender. I'm eight."

"I'm eight too!" said Éclair.

"And I'm Nettle and I'm nine!"

"Lavender's my sister," explained Blueberry.

"Oh cool!" said Éclair. "Do you fancy a game of tag?"

Tag was Éclair's favourite game, and fortunately the rules are identical across all dimensions. It's quite possibly the most parallel element in existence.

As expected, the young dragons were game and hours passed before Éclair gave anything else a second thought. It wasn't until they lay down giggling in exhaustion that Éclair remembered why she was here.

"Oh no!!" she gasped. "I've got to go! I forgot all about Carlos! I have to take him to Unicorn Mountain. Do you know where it is?"

"Hmmm…" Bluebell pondered. "I think so. I saw him running away earlier and he looked like he was running back towards the mountains. Did you see the big purple cliffs earlier?" The dragons chattered excitedly about where they had last seen Unicorn Mountain, and Éclair was finally clear on where to go.

"Thanks so much! You guys are brilliant!"

"That's ok!" said Bluebell. "Be careful though, you need to sneak up on him. He's really scared of dragons."

"Yeah…" sighed Éclair. "I think he was running away from me earlier. I didn't mean to scare him!"

The other dragons laughed, and explained they had all done the same in the past.

"I guess I should go now, Carlos will be wondering where I am."

"Well it was nice playing with you," said Bluebell. "Are you sure you can't stay for tea?"

"I'd love to," she replied, "but I really have to go now, I'm going to be in so much trouble. Can I come another day though?"

"Of course!!" said Blueberry, "you have to!"

"And can I bring my friends?"

"Yes!" the dragons chorused excitedly. "We want to hear all about your adventures again!"

As Éclair flew away from the dragon land in the clouds, her new friends circled around her. She was left with cries of "Good luck!" and "Come again soon!" ringing in her ears. All of a sudden Éclair felt she could be really at home here.

It wasn't long before she spotted the wood that she had left Carlos sleeping by, and she flew down towards him.

"Éclair! Where've you been?!" scolded Carlos who was panicking slightly. Not only had he been worried about Éclair, but he needed her to get to Unicorn Mountain quickly. They had agreed to have a rest, but not one which meant that Dr Funk had loads of time to catch up with them. The last thing he wanted was for him to get to Unicorn Mountain before they did.

"I'm sorry Carlos," Éclair replied, looking guiltily at her feet. "I found some other dragons and I went to see their home. It's really cool. It's up in the clouds, and there are hundreds, thousands, no millions of dragons! They're all different colours, and I saw waterfalls, and I played tag with Blueberry and Nettle and..."

"You've been **playing** whilst I've been worrying about how we are going to find Maria before Dr Funk does?" Carlos gave Éclair a look of amazement.

"I'm sorry!" cried Éclair, bursting into tears and

splattering cream all over Carlos.

Carlos instantly regretted scolding Éclair. She was eight years old, she was just doing what eight year olds do. And given what she had been through, she did deserve a bit of fun to take her mind off it.

"Hey, don't worry Éclair. I'm sorry, I shouldn't have shouted. I'm glad you had a good time and made some friends."

Éclair stopped her sniffling and listened to Carlos.

"I do think we need to go straight away though, just in case Dr Funk is around. I think we should head over that way – that seems to be the direction he was running in earlier."

"No it's not there Carlos. Don't worry, I know the way to Unicorn Mountain."

"You do?" Carlos was astounded.

"Yep," said Éclair. "My friends saw him running away after we saw him earlier. Apparently he's really scared of dragons. We need to fly along the coast, turn right at the purple cliffs, fly along the river until we see the big rainforest to the left and he will be somewhere around there."

"Well done Éclair!" cried Carlos. "You're a star!"

Forgetting her tears of a few minutes ago and beaming at his praise, Éclair and Carlos flew up in to the sky, once more in search of Unicorn Mountain.

CHAPTER 35

Maria and the others approached the Unicorn Mountain, Reginald. He was crying and shaking vigorously.

"Erm... Reginald?" Maria called loudly.

"Don't speak to him!!!" hissed Pete. "Can't you see he's upset?!"

It was too late.

"Go away!" shouted Reginald, who had stood, ready to flee if Maria and her friends didn't.

The group stood still, unsure what to do.

"Sing!" instructed Pete. "It's the only chance!"

The group of friends looked at each other. Nobody knew if any of the others could sing.

"Quickly! If he bolts, we might never get close to him again!"

Maria took it on herself to sing, she had to try. If Reginald did run off, his long legs would take him hundreds of miles away within minutes. Maria wasn't the most confident songstress, but the alternatives didn't seem great. She couldn't imagine a pink hyena being any good, Gladys was definitely a squawker and she could only imagine that Steve's singing would make the unicorn suicidal.

Choosing a traditional Mexican song that Carlos liked, she began.

After a couple of lines she thought that Reginald had stopped sobbing, which was a definite improvement. She thought it now unlikely that he would run away, but she still needed to impress him enough that they could climb Unicorn Mountain to meet Carlos. She continued, nervously, but when she got to the final chorus knew she had nailed it. Sparkles joined in, a deep and emotional tenor voice cutting effortlessly through the air. *I bet he wouldn't sound like that with his springs on,* she thought.

Nonetheless, they finished to an air of silence save the sound of Steve sobbing in the background. "That was beautiful!" he cried. None of them had ever heard a depressed tortoise crying before and they weren't sure they ever wanted to again. It was a strange sound, like an asthmatic porcupine falling off a bridge and landing spikes down on an operatic kitten.

Maria looked at Reginald hopefully.

"That was amazing!" said a lilting voice from across the valleys.

Maria looked around for the source. *It must be Reginald,* she thought, *but that voice sounds like it could be coming from anywhere. Or everywhere!*

"I would love to clap," he continued "but I have hooves and I don't like to clop. The other unicorns get excited and think I'm coming to visit."

"Other unicorns?" asked Maria. "Are there more unicorns here?"

"Oh no, not here," answered Reginald. "They're in

other dimensions. Us unicorns are magical and can fly across them using the art of clopping."

"You can fly to other dimensions?! That's astonishing!" said Maria. This news brightened her up even more than reaching Unicorn Mountain. *He might be able to take us home!*

"We also have magical voices," said Reginald. "I saw you looking a little bit disorientated when I first spoke. That's because our voices have built-in ventriloquist properties – it helps us to talk to each other from far, far away without deafening the rest of the world."

Maria nodded, that did explain a lot.

"Anyway," said Reginald. "I've never seen you here before. Have you come to climb Unicorn Mountain?"

Maria explained that they were actually from another dimension and they were meeting her boyfriend Carlos at the top. "It's the only place we knew about," she continued. "Will you make sure you let him come up? He won't know that he has to sing, and he's terrible!"

"Yes, of course I will!" Reginald enthused. "I can't wait to meet your boyfriend, the one who inspires you to sing so beautifully!"

Maria was relieved. She understood why Unicorn Mountain had been the clear landmark identified in the book Carlos had, but they hadn't realised it would be so difficult to even start hiking up! It was great that Carlos would be allowed on, no questions asked, once he got there.

They thanked Pete the Uniman for his help getting to Unicorn Mountain, before a magical wind whisked them into the air, floating towards the winding path which spiralled gradually upwards around Reginald's leg.

The travellers landed just above his front left hoof,

leaving Pete the Uniman waving to them from the solid ground below.

"Come back for tea whenever you want!" he called as they all waved back gratefully.

As the travellers began to climb the white, hairy path around Reginald's calf, the unicorn stood and began to trot away on his usual route around the kingdom.

CHAPTER 36

After a few hours of gruelling hiking along Reginald's leg, the sun was beginning to set and Maria was starting to get a little worried about where they were going to sleep. She couldn't even ask Reginald what to do. He'd gone awfully quiet and she assumed that he was having a sleep himself.

Despite her calmness and the fact that she was taking everything in her stride, she didn't particularly like having to sleep rough under the stars. Fortunately though, she spotted a small cave in the distance where they might be able to take refuge for the night.

On entering what looked like a little recess in Reginald's fur they were greeted with a whiff of smoke which appeared to be coming from a tunnel hidden in the back corner. Hoping that they might find people and somewhere warm to sleep, they followed the winding passage into the heart of the mountain.

The smell of smoke was getting stronger, and Maria could also detect other fragrances – spices and roasting meat. This encouraged them even further! It had been a long time since the tea party and the walking had made them quite peckish[28].

As they rounded the next corner, there was a small fire with a spit roasting above it. A small bearded old man was sitting next to it, cross-legged on the floor. Relieved and excited to see a fellow human, Maria went straight across to greet him.

"Shsssh," scolded the old man instantly as she opened her mouth to say "hello". She was a little taken about, but not one to be easily put off, Maria waited patiently before she tried again.

"Hi," she said politely. "We're walking up Unicorn Mountain, but I think we started too late in the day, so we're in need of somewhere to rest for the night."

The old man glared and said sharply, "I'm cooking. Please be quiet until my tea is finished."

Maria sat quietly by the fire next to the grumpy old man, and Gladys, Sparkles and Steve joined her. Literally two seconds later the old man cried "Finished!" bounding in a sprightly fashion to his feet to remove the spit from the fire. He noisily began to rip the meat off with his teeth, seemingly oblivious to the hungry stares of those around him. Despite burning his mouth a couple of times, he finished his meal off quickly and turned to face Maria with an inquisitive look on his face.

"So, what do we have here?" he asked rhetorically before continuing. "Ahhh yes. I knew you'd come along eventually." He studied every inch of Maria's face in great detail, boring into her brown eyes and casting a glance over her long curls. "Yes. Maria isn't it?" Dumbfounded as she hadn't introduced herself but he

---

28   Especially Gladys. Groan...

already knew her name, Maria nodded, before the strange man repeated the feat with the other members of her little group.

"You're late you know. I'm quite disappointed really, it's just bad manners. You're usually so reliable compared to the others. I assume it was **his** fault," he said, casting an accusatory glance at Steve.

"I'm sorry," replied Maria, completely confused but remaining polite. They needed somewhere to stay after all and they hadn't any other options. "So... how do you know all about us already? Have you been speaking to Reginald?"

Conversation with the unicorn did seem like a logical way for the old man to be so well informed, so Maria was shocked when he shook his head.

"No. I am Ridley, and I see you in the flames," he whispered, waving his arms towards the fire dramatically. "They tell me things, and warn me of things to come. You have an interesting life ahead of you, young Maria. In the flames I have seen some goodness, but I have also seen some dire deeds, and I have but one message for you all at this time. Trust not the one they call Carlos, he is not as he seems! Beware of him or you will find yourself in grave danger."

"Carlos?!" questioned Sparkles. "We can trust Carlos, he helped us get here." He looked at Maria who agreed wholeheartedly.

"Yes! He is my Carlos! I know he's not perfect, but he'd do nothing to hurt any of us."

"And so you may believe," continued Ridley, shaking his head vigorously. "But you must heed my warning! My foresights are always true. Beware of this Carlos tomorrow, do not trust him."

"We are seeing Carlos tomorrow?!" squawked Gladys, who like everyone else was pleased and not at all worried about the prospect of his return. With the exception of Steve, of course, who was chuntering away to himself.

"Great. Even Carlos hates us now. This is brilliant. When are we going to get a break?"

Frustrated that the group weren't going to take his warning seriously, Ridley told the group that they were free to sleep around the fire, and he stomped off to bed muttering about the "stupid headstrong youth of today... too proud to heed my warnings..."

"Ridley!" Maria called, and he turned and looked at her. "What happens to us? What should we do?"

Ridley gave her a glare that summed up how he felt about their dismissal of his visions. They wouldn't be getting any more out of Ridley tonight.

The hungry group spread out around the warm flames. Sleep came easily to them all, after the tiring day they'd had. Everyone slept through, dreaming of being united with Carlos and generally feeling positive about the day ahead.

They had a rude awakening the following morning though, with an early wake up thanks to the ground shaking violently. Remembering her experience in Lemon Drizzle's shopping centre, Maria wasn't too worried.

"It's just Reginald having a run around," she assured the others, who believed her with little fuss. They'd all survived it there too. Even so, nobody left the protection of the cave until the shaking stopped.

The group were getting frustrated though. They were looking forward to the prospect of seeing Carlos later on and they sat around fidgeting, desperate to get on with their hike to the top. The moment it was safe to do so, they would get going once more.

CHAPTER 37

Carlos and Éclair flew around the panic stricken unicorn, who whinnied and dodged the cake dragon. Éclair called out to him, trying to calm him, but this only made things worse. Reginald was so scared of Éclair that she couldn't get anywhere near him. Eventually, worried that the unicorn was bucking so much that he might fall over and hurt himself, Éclair and Carlos flew away and hid, out of his line of sight.

"Well how are we going to get to Maria now?" asked Éclair. "The unicorn is so scared of me that I can't get anywhere near him."

"I'm not sure," said Carlos. "Maybe we can try to sneak up on him later when he's settled, and if that doesn't work then I might have to go by myself," suggested Carlos.

"But I'll be all alone!" said Éclair, visibly upset. Carlos was finding being a cake dragon's stand in parent quite challenging.

"Oh yeah! I forgot that. You could always go and play with your new dragon friends for a bit if that happened though." Éclair seemed to brighten up a little at the thought.

"But don't worry," Carlos continued. "It probably won't come to that anyway!"

To make Éclair feel better, they sat chatting for a few hours, hatching a variety of cunning plans they could use to sneak up Unicorn Mountain and find Maria.

CHAPTER 38

Due to the helpful nature of its inhabitants, Dr Funk had quickly found his way around the Kingdom of Happiness and All Things Warm and Fluffy. Given Carlos's recognition of it when they landed here, he had correctly assumed that he would be meeting Maria at Unicorn Mountain, the most obvious landmark. That meant that Gladys, Dr Funk's Ultimate Weapon, would be there too. He rubbed his hands together in anticipation, he was so looking forward to being reunited!

Dr Funk was waiting patiently at Unicorn Mountain Boarding Stop 15A, where it wouldn't be long before the unicorn arrived so that he could board and begin his ascent to revenge.

It was quite easy to be patient. Dr Funk was sitting in the Valley of the Vacant, a huge open grassy expanse where he could see for miles around. Reginald was clearly visible in the far distance so Dr Funk knew he was approaching. Eventually, Reginald arrived and spoke to Dr Funk.

"Well hello," lilted Reginald happily. He had been in a terrific mood ever since Maria and Sparkles had serenaded him so beautifully. "And who do we have here?"

"Hi," said Dr Funk. "I'm Carlos."

"Carlos!" Reginald exclaimed. Dr Funk almost swooned. An exclamation from a unicorn sounds like a thousand wind chimes floating down from heaven, carried by a choir of humming angels with tinsel on their wings. It's well known in the Outer Dimensions that a man who doesn't weaken at the knees from a unicorn exclamation has the hardest of hard hearts. They're the kind of men that go to hospital for a heart bypass and actually have a tarmac road put in.

"Well say no more! You don't have to sing or tell me any stories, your wonderful Maria has already done more than enough. Welcome to Unicorn Mountain! Make haste to the top where you will be reunited with your friends."

Gleefully, Dr Funk floated upwards towards Reginald's back hoof. Reginald was a maze of trodden paths but it appeared Dr Funk had landed on one of the longest ones. He had to make his way not only up Reginald's long and meaty leg, but along his back, around his mane and over his head. Dr Funk assumed that they would be meeting on his head. Or even on his horn! That must be the summit, surely!

For both parties it was a long and gruelling climb upwards, made better by the bits of dialogue passed between themselves and Reginald.

Maria spent ages telling Reginald about her home dimension, and he was very interested, asking all kinds of questions. She was equally excited to tell him about her home. Knowing that unicorns could travel and talk across dimensions had given her renewed hope that she might find her way home. Unfortunately, Reginald didn't know any unicorns who recognised her descriptions, which disappointed Maria greatly. It was a different matter when Sparkles told Reginald about his home though.

"Strange things happened to my home before we left, Reginald. I wonder if you'd know anything about it. We were all inside in my former master's laboratory, and when we came out the whole landscape had changed! It was once a dry, arid land, rocky and brown and boring. The home that Dr Funk had made for us was one of the only inhabitable places on my planet. But when we came out, it was pink, and there was a flowing river, and candy cane trees. Quite a transformation."

"Really? That's very strange. What was the name of your dimension?"

"I... I don't know. We never spoke in terms of dimensions, we didn't know one could travel outside of them until now! Carlos appeared in ours from somewhere called Pink River though."

"Pink River...ah yes! I don't know of a dimension called Pink River, but my cousin did meet some dragons from a town called Pink River the other day. I remember this distinctly because two dimensions merged together, and then the one outside of it exploded! Anyway, it was all a bit crazy, and lots of people ended up in domarn places. These poor dragons had been left sitting on the side of a football pitch in a dimension called Wemberley."

Although it was sad that they had been uprooted from their home, Maria saw the bright side of the news.

At least we know where to look for Éclair's parents, she thought, *if she hasn't already found them.*

"Incidentally," continued Reginald, "you might be pleased to know that a certain Carlos has just started to climb Unicorn Mountain."

Maria jumped for joy, and the spirits of the whole group visibly lifted.

"That's excellent news! Tell him we'll see him at the top!"

There were beaming smiles all around. Steve even managed to walk at a normal walking pace for around five minutes.

Likewise, hearing that Maria and her friends could not wait to see him filled the Carlos impersonator, Dr Funk, with glee.

"Not as much as I'm looking forward to seeing you, my beautiful Gladys," he thought, rubbing the jar of apricot jam he kept in his lab-coat pocket for exactly this kind of situation.

CHAPTER 39

Despite having a much longer hike up Unicorn Mountain, Dr Funk made it to the top of Reginald's head a long time before Maria and the others did. Amazed by the view, he thought he could see the whole kingdom from up there. Stretching out into the distance was a vast rainforest, the same one which Maria and the others had hiked through. Alongside the rainforest was a mountain region, with its steep inclines edging long and expansive valleys. The other side of the kingdom was a sharp contrast. There was a large urban settlement, which looked busy and lively with its moving crowds and bustling colours. The tightly packed buildings looked intriguing, brightly decorated in all sorts of shapes and sizes. Some didn't even look like traditional buildings, he could have sworn one was a lemon. Still, it was a sight just to behold the friendly clutter and vibrancy the city seemed to emanate.

Dr Funk was almost sad that he wouldn't get to experience it.

Having decided that he wanted his moment of perfect revenge to be at the summit, Dr Funk walked over to Reginald's horn and started the slippery walk along the conical[29] ridge. A few cautious slips and slides later he made it to the very end, the horn's point, where he sat with his feet dangling over the edge.

Feeling strangely at ease with himself, Dr Funk sat, reflecting on his life.

It had been a tough one. A bad upbringing, which had filled him with hate and rage. A desire for revenge which had taken over his life, but had so far remained unfulfilled. He was never going to get his revenge on Sandwich, that much had eluded him, but he sure wasn't going to fail with Carlos. Carlos, the man who had ruined the carefully laid plans he had spent his whole life working towards.

Yes, Dr Funk would love to destroy Carlos, but there was only one way he could hurt him more than killing him. That's right - by taking his Maria away from him.

Grinning slyly to himself he thought about Gladys and the torch. A lifetime had been spent conducting experiments, creating a vessel of evil. And now he had done it. Gladys, the product of the Torch of Darkness that Carlos had stolen, was his Ultimate Weapon and he could not wait to see his experiment succeed. In fact he was so busy dwelling on his success, and dreaming about his moment of triumph that he nearly failed to notice Maria and the others approaching.

"Carlos!" shouted Sparkles, seeing Dr Funk's figure in the distance.

---

29   Conical. A unicorn's horn is no laughing matter.

Laughing to himself, Dr Funk turned and waved. They waved back.

This is my moment, he thought. *Revenge is nigh.*

Matty Millard

CHAPTER 40

Reginald had reached another stop, where the real Carlos was waiting, alone.

A second attempt to sneak up on Reginald with Éclair had already caused Reginald to bolt, and Carlos wasn't willing to risk that happening again. It had been a long time since they had seen Dr Funk, and Carlos knew he needed to get to Maria before Dr Funk did. The need for this to happen quickly was more urgent than he might know, but Carlos wasn't taking any risks anyway. Carlos would be ascending Unicorn Mountain by himself.

Reginald greeted Carlos in his usual polite manner, asking him who he was and why he was here.

"Hi! I'm Carlos, and I'm here to see my girlfriend, Maria," explained Carlos. "We're meeting at the top of the mountain... Erm... What's your name?" Carlos felt a bit silly but he didn't know what else to ask a talking mountain.

"Hmmm..." said Reginald thoughtfully. He knelt down and brought his giant pointed head slowly towards

Carlos, staring at him closely.

"It's you!" he spat suddenly. "Get away! You're that horrible man with the dragon! Carlos is already here, you imposter!"

With that Reginald stood and wandered off angrily, chuntering to himself and stamping his back feet.

For a minute Carlos was puzzled. *He thinks I'm already on the mountain? What's he talking about?* And then it hit him. There could only be one explanation - Dr Funk.

"ÉCLAIR!" bellowed Carlos urgently. The cake dragon appeared from hiding instantly. "We have to get on there somehow, and quickly!"

"Don't worry!" came a high pitched cry from the skies. "We can help!"

Blueberry, Nettle and Lavender landed next to Éclair and excited dragon chatter filled the air. Carlos wasn't quite sure whether this was a good or a bad thing.

CHAPTER 41

They were around 30 feet apart when Dr Funk got up from the mountain's edge and walked towards Maria and her friends.

"Lovely to see you all," he declared, revelling in the shocked and fearful expressions on their faces.

"Sparkles, I like the look. It's far more sophisticated that those primitive springs you used to bounce around on. And Steve, my head guard. It's just not been the same without you. I always felt, so....so superior with you useless creatures around." Dr Funk looked around the group slowly, an irritating smirk on his face. "I suppose, in a strange kind of way, I might even have missed you."

Dr Funk paused dramatically. This was his revenge, his theatre, and he was going to make the most of it.

"Especially you, my dearest Gladys. I've been looking everywhere for you." He smiled manically towards his Ultimate Weapon, who was backing away from him, eyes wide with fear. Her wood snake arms were alive and hissing at him.

"What do you want?" shouted Sparkles. "Why can't you just leave us alone?"

Maria had been stopped in her tracks, she didn't know what to do. She was actually quite glad that Sparkles had taken charge of the situation.

Dr Funk just laughed.

"You heard him!" shouted Maria. "Go away! We're not doing you any harm!" she protested.

Dr Funk's face went black with rage.

"Not done me any harm? Not done me any HARM?!" he bellowed.

"You've STOLEN from me! You stole my Torch of Darkness! You put a giant hole in the roof of my laboratory which I can no longer get to because of you! You've stolen my guards! You've stolen my experiments..." he looked towards Steve, Gladys and Sparkles with a hint of sadness and an air of madness. "And not only have you stolen my experiments, my whole life's work, you have destroyed my goals and made the one thing I have wanted to achieve **impossible!** So now, in the place of Sandwich, you are going to pay!"

The friends froze as Dr Funk reached into his pocket.

"They didn't do any of that, I did," announced Carlos, flying in on the back of Éclair and landing next to Maria. Three other brightly coloured dragons landed around him. Third time lucky, thanks to Éclair's dragon friends who knew and distracted the unicorn with their chatter, Éclair had managed to sneak past Reginald's watchful eye and fly in on his blind side.

"And nobody will be paying for anything - except for you."

Far from being dismayed, Dr Funk was happy that

Carlos was there. This was exactly the situation he had dreamed about.

"That's what you think," he said, unscrewing the lid from the jar of apricot jam. Carlos shouted a warning as Dr Funk launched the jar towards Gladys.

It was a good shot. The jam went everywhere, all over Gladys and her wood snakes.

There was a huge explosion.

Matty Millard

CHAPTER 42

Reginald whinnied in panic, rose up onto his two hind legs and cantered off in a rmdnao direction. An explosion in the face tends to have that effect on creatures of an equine nature.

"Reginald!" heard all the inhabitants of the Valley of the Vacant[30] as a voice tinkled around the valley with the delicateness of the first dew of spring.

"Reginald! Calm down!" repeated the voice.

"There there, Reginald. It'll be fine. Take a deep

---

30 Which clearly wasn't many, hence the name. It must be pointed out that it's not a vacant valley, as it often contains a gigantic unicorn – the same one that was running around in a mad panic following the aforementioned explosion. No, the vacant bit describes the people. Their vacancy is surmised by the fact that they stand on the slopes of the valley, watching. That's it. They stand and watch life go by, eyes bulging, mouth wide open, completely transfixed. At this moment in time it was probably quite an interesting thing to do, but usually it just distracted them from important tasks like eating, drinking, reproducing and sleeping. The lack of which had resulted in, well, a vacant valley, thanks to the Vacant.

breath."

Reginald was still in a state of panic, words wouldn't help.

A brief, tinkly argument echoed around before one exasperated voice conceded. *"Fine, I'll do it, but it's your turn next time."*

The unicorn song that followed can only be defined as the most incredible sound you can ever dream of hearing. I'm not even going to try and describe it, but basically everyone who heard it temporarily lost their mind. Most fell to their knees, some leapt up and rejoiced. Basalt, the much decorated God of Geology wept for forty days and forty nights. Tears had never come from his stony eyes before, and they flooded the kitchen worktop that he had been made into.

"He came through worlds and ages past,
Courageous, strong and free,
He brought us gifts and tales and laughs,
Corinthius was he.

He'd rode the clouds, he'd won the wars,
He'd rescued maidens fair,
Corinthius, he used all fours,
To triumph everywhere.

Our teacher, friend and stable hand,
Pioneer of our race,
He taught us of our magics, and
We clopped around the place.

So evermore we'll use our horn,
And the powers it provides,
I'll practice with it every morn,
To keep his memory alive."

Reginald's favourite song, a ballad in honour of Corinthius, the most celebrated unicorn in history, was enough to capture his attention and calm him down. By the end of the song the exhausted unicorn had lay down in a field and fallen fast asleep.

On the top of Reginald's head, Carlos scanned the scene as the ground stopped shaking and the black smoke dissipated.

"Maria!" he called. "Are you alright?"

"Yes!" she shouted, running over to Carlos and hugging him, but withdrawing instantly at his touch. "But you're not, you're burning hot! And there's smoke coming out of your ears!"

Carlos looked at his hands. They were bright red but lessening by the minute.

Éclair blew some squirty cream at him which sizzled but cooled him down a little.

"Thanks, I think," smiled Carlos who could hear Éclair's dragon friends flying around chattering with excitement overhead. *They won't stop talking about this for years,* he supposed.

A little shaken, a bit confused about his burning hands, but feeling ok otherwise, Carlos looked around to see how the others were. Sparkles was on his feet, limping a little but groaning in a civilised manner.

"Steve!" he called as he knocked on Steve's shell. The tortoise had sensibly withdrawn into it by instinct at the sound of the explosion. "Steve! You ok?"

There was no reply, and Sparkles swapped a worried look with Carlos.

He tried knocking one more time. "Steve? You in there?"

"No," answered Steve. "Go and bother me in my other house, the one that isn't in the middle of a war zone."

Maria laughed. "Steve's fine then!"

They decided to leave him for a while, there was no doubting that a large explosion would make Steve even more grumpy than usual.

Sitting next to Steve was a ruffled looking Gladys, using her wood snake arms to pat down her feathers.

"Gladys!" Carlos exclaimed. "You're ok?!"

"I am!" said Gladys. "And so are you!"

"But... but you just exploded!"

"What?" squawked Gladys, looking at Carlos as if he was stupid. "No I didn't. I'm here, look! All in one piece!"

"But..." Carlos was out of words and he didn't want to say the ones he was thinking. *You're Dr Funk's Ultimate Weapon! If you hadn't exploded, what had?*

Carlos knew he wasn't imagining it. There had definitely been an explosion, because the end of poor Reginald's horn had been blown off. Dr Funk must have fallen with it as there was no sign of him anywhere. That was more than likely as he had been stood quite close to the edge when he threw the jam at Gladys.

Satisfied that everyone was unhurt, the friends sat around recovering in silence. A bit of quiet was the least they deserved after the few days they had had. Maria dozed with her head resting on Carlos's shoulder. She was glad to have him back, and she wouldn't be letting him go again for a long, long time.

But Carlos was still pondering over the day's events. He hated the unknown, there had to be a rational explanation for all this. How had Gladys not blown up? It didn't make any sense! Eventually, he forced himself to put it to the back of his mind. *Does it really matter what happened? Dr Funk is gone, and now we're all safe. That's by far the most important thing.*

After a good sleep, everyone had got a bit of energy back, except for the dragons who were still playing together. Even Steve had popped his head out of his shell for a tentative look around.

They all sat up when they heard a loud buzzing and a crackle.

"What was that?" asked Maria.

They sat in complete silence. A few seconds later they heard it again.

"I knew it wasn't over," said Steve. "Dr Funk's coming after us again…"

Nobody dared to say any different, and Carlos had leapt to his feet, fists readied for a fight.

CHAPTER 43

The friends stood in a circle, watching the strange shimmering in the air in front of them. No-one knew what was going on, but one thing was for sure, they all expected the worst.

The feeling of dread heightened when two figures walked out of the shimmering air, and came towards them.

"Maria!" cried one of them.

Carlos dropped his fists, relieved.

"Terrence!!" shouted Maria and rushed towards her brother who had a coat-hanger wrapped around his head. "Are you ok? What happened?"

"I'm fine…" said Terrence.

"I knew I shouldn't have let you go off by yourself, even in a shopping centre. You know you've done this before don't you? When you were ten, you got lost in…"

"I didn't get lost!" interrupted Terrence, exasperated.

"Yes you did!" laughed Maria. "Mom and Dad found you hung up on a rack of jeans!"

"Strangely enough," interjected Lemon Drizzle,

"that's exactly where I found him this time."

"Thanks for bringing him back," Maria said, beaming at Lemon, "it's much appreciated."

She gave him a warm hug, which she instantly regretted when she had to wrestle her way free of his grasp. She stood back, trying to avoid his longing stare.

"That's ok darling," Lemon replied. "I assume my heroics mean that you'll be taking me out on a date to say thank you?"

Before she could say no, he pulled her back towards him, and puckered his lips up.

Maria had him pinned him to the floor in an instant, his arm twisted behind his back. Carlos was impressed, if a little scared.

"I don't think so," she said. "You're far too creepy. Thanks for bringing Terrence back, but I have my Carlos. The only chance you have of ever seeing me again is if I need some new clothes and I come back to Unicorn Hill."

She released Lemon, who stood up and brushed himself down calmly.

"Oh, you'll need more clothes. They always do," he muttered, almost to himself. "In that case, it's a date. I'll be waiting for you. You'll be sick of this good-for-nothing loser soon enough. See you soon, my honey."

With that, the super-confident Lemon Drizzle disappeared into the air and the group were complete once more.

"I didn't get lost…" muttered Terrence, hoping that somebody might listen to his side of the story. "He trapped me!"

"Urgggh…" said Maria, shivering a little. "I could do with a cuppa after all that."

CHAPTER 44

"Reginald!" shouted Sparkles. "Wake up!"

"Reginald!" chorused everyone.

The friends had made their way back down to the bottom of the path they had ascended, which meant they were sitting on the top of Reginald's hoof. Below them was a sheer drop to the floor of The Kingdom of Happiness and All Things Warm and Fluffy. The magical wind that had lifted them up had not come to take them back down again, and they were pretty sure that was because Reginald was asleep.

"Éclair!" shouted Carlos. The cake dragon had gone for a fly with her friends and predictably they were playing tag in the sky. She heard Carlos though and came to fly them down to the ground where they all looked worriedly at Reginald.

"What can we do?" said Maria. "Who can look after an ill Unicorn? We can't just leave him alone by himself while we go and find help. This is all our fault too, Dr Funk was after us! What if he doesn't wake up for years and years like last time? What if... what if he doesn't wake up at all?"

Carlos put a comforting arm around Maria. They all felt the same. Reginald had been nothing but friendly towards them, and it was due to Dr Funk's attempt on their life that he was in this state.

"I'm going to punch him on the nose," said Terrence.

"What?" said Carlos. "Why? He's a mountain, he won't even feel that!"

"Yes he will," replied Terrence. "If a punch on the nose is enough to fight a shark attack, then it's enough to wake up a unicorn."

To say Maria and Carlos were astounded was an underestimate. Terrence having an idea was rare enough, but Terrence volunteering to carry out his idea was a completely different kettle of fish. Although, punching an unconscious unicorn on the nose is probably not an act that will ever be rewarded with medals for bravery.

The group walked the short distance to Reginald's face and stood by.

"At least we know he's breathing," said Maria. It was clear from the air being sucked and blown from Reginald nose that he was definitely alive. She made sure she was well out of range, she had no intention of being splattered with whatever might get blown out of a unicorn's nose when asleep.

Terrence crept up to Reginald on his toes. Quite why he did that nobody knew, the whole aim was to wake him after all. However, this was Terrence's plan and he would do it his way.

Standing as tall as he could, but still dwarfed next to Reginald's pure white nose, was Terrence. He set himself, scrunched his fist into a ball and looked away from Reginald. He was going to put his all into this.

Carlos was trying his hardest not to laugh. It was the most ridiculous thing he'd ever seen.

Terrence span on the spot, and threw a right hook at the unicorn. It hit, and he shook his hand at the pain from the impact.

Much to the astonishment of everyone, Reginald stirred.

His eyelid flickered, and a look of irritation flashed across his face. He let out a murmur, and nuzzled his face into the ground.

Terrence gave his friends a look that would have silenced the noisiest doubter.

"See! I told you he would feel it! I can wake him up this time!"

Terrence repeated his little ritual, span, and struck the unicorn again.

This time, there was a louder and longer murmur. Reginald opened his mouth and began to snore.

"Help!!!" screamed Terrence as he was sucked in by Reginald's first deep breath.

Maria and Carlos began to run to help him as Terrence staggered towards Reginald. Unable to brace himself against the force of his breathing, Terrence splattered onto Reginald's bottom gum where he stuck with a squelch in the sticky saliva. Terrence stayed there, helpless, through a couple of snores, before he was spat out towards them on a particularly loud snore out.

The look of embarrassment on Terrence's face even brought a brief smile from Steve.

"I think we should go now," said the dripping Terrence, but nobody really heard him. It was a good ten minutes before the dragons stopped rolling around in hysterics. The four of them were like an infinite domino chain of laughter.

"Let's go and find Pete," said Maria when the noise had quietened down. "He'll know what to do. There must be someone in this land that can help unicorns."

There were no arguments, and so they held on tightly as Éclair flew them away from Reginald. As they left they saw a couple of unicorns shimmer into existence next to him.

"He's got friends!" Maria exclaimed. "I'm so glad there's someone here to look after him. Let's go and rest now, we'll come back to apologise another day when he's awake."

Satisfied that Reginald was in capable hands, the friends went in search of the accommodating Unimen they had met when they first arrived in the Kingdom of Happiness and All Things Warm and Fluffy.

CHAPTER 45

After a few days of wandering around the rainforest, hoping to be kidnapped into a tea party, they finally came upon Pete.

"Hi Maria!" he said. "Have you come back for another tea party?!"

"Yes please!" she declared. "We've been looking for you for days!"

"Have you?" replied Pete. "We did see you walking around but we weren't sure whether you wanted one or not. Especially after last time, you know, when you thought you were being kidnapped."

"Oh Pete," she giggled. "You're so funny, you should have just come and spoken to us!"

Pete put his arm in the air as a signal and the party was quickly ambushed by the Unimen and dragged into the tea-rooms.

Well at least they asked this time, thought Maria.

Once they were inside, Sparkles collapsed to the floor.

"Pete," he began. "Do you mind if I take my shoes

off? My feet are killing me!"

Pete shook his head, so Sparkles set upon the arduous task of unlacing his massive pink platforms and sighed in relief as he did so. As soon as he removed them to reveal the set of springs on his feet, he jumped up and screeched "Iiiiiiiiiii'm at a tea-partyyyyyy! Wheeeeeeeee!" As he ricocheted off the cave walls, Pete signalled to his Unimen to put the best china away and get the old stuff out. Everyone laughed, it was nice to have the old Sparkles back.

The tea party was so welcomed by the travellers that Steve didn't even moan about the triangular sandwiches. For the first time in ages, they sat happily chatting about Dr Funk, Unicorn Mountain and everything else that had happened over the past few weeks. No-one worried about a thing in the world.

"I'm tired," said Carlos, "but I've got quite a good feeling about this place." Maria nodded in agreement.

Carlos continued. "How would you feel if we stayed here for a while? I'm fed up of constantly running away from danger, and it should be fine here now that Dr Funk's gone."

"I don't like it," said Steve.

Carlos sighed. "Why does that not surprise me?"

"I don't know," said Steve. "Maybe you should be surprised. I don't like it because as well as being attacked by Dr Funk we got chased by a crazy guy with a gun. And I fell in a hole. It doesn't seem very safe to me."

"Oh yes!" exclaimed Maria. "I had forgotten all about Clive!"

"He was nasty," said Gladys, her wood snakes hissing in agreement.

Pete had been very quiet so far, but he had perked up

at the name Clive. "Clive, you say? Would this by any chance be a green lizard, often found walking around in a suit?"

"That's the one!" said Maria. "He chased us with a gun!"

Pete laughed. "That happens all the time, he'll never learn."

The group were paying full attention so he continued.

"Clive is a toymaker," explained Pete. "He makes toys, and gives them away to the poor kids. We've told him to tell people what he does, you wouldn't believe the amount of people who've reported him for waving swords at them and the like."

"Really?" said Maria. "But that's really nice! Why doesn't he want people to know?"

Again, Pete laughed. "He thinks he's working for a higher deity. He keeps his toy-making secret, mysterious amounts of Ochres appear through his door. Everyone knows he does it and people make him anonymous donations. He thinks it's God's way of rewarding him for his kindness. It's not though, it's us."

"That's nice though," agreed Maria. "As long as it works, why should he know any different?"

"Exactly," Pete nodded.

"So do we have a decision?" asked Carlos. "Are we staying?"

A loud chorus of "YES!" answered that one.

"And maybe one day when he's better," said Maria, "we can speak to Reginald about the best way to find our way home. Maybe one of his unicorn friends might help us travel there. But for now, we'll stay. I think I like it here."

The friends were all in agreement and tucked into a

second round of sandwiches.

"This is really nice," said Gladys, taking a bite out of a wholemeal triangle. "What is it?"

"Nothing special, it's just home-made apricot jam," said Pete, to the horror of Carlos and the others who dove under the table instinctively.

A tense silence followed, but there was no explosion.

"Have you eaten it?" asked Carlos before he dared to come out from under cover.

Gladys's response of "yes, all of it," filled him with the confidence that as Gladys hadn't blown up, she probably wouldn't blow up.

"Carlos!" exclaimed Maria. "You've got smoke coming out of your ears!"

Just as he had done at the top of Unicorn Mountain, Carlos was burning up, and he continued to heat up whilst Gladys's wood snakes licked out a jam pot.

Suddenly it dawned on him.

Gladys hadn't exploded after all, it was Dr Funk who had exploded! As usual, his experiment had been a total failure. Instead of creating a weapon which would explode on contact with apricot jam, he'd created one whose maker would! Anyone who had used the torch Dr Funk had made would be in danger of explosion. Thankfully, Carlos had only used it for a few minutes on the wood snakes, which must be why he had merely smoked a little.

Even so, Carlos would be keeping Gladys and those wood snakes as far away from apricot jam as he could in future. He didn't want to be burning people or setting things on fire by accident.

And with that mystery solved, they spoke to Pete at

length about the Kingdom of Happiness and All Things Warm and Fluffy. Where could they live, how could they get jobs, and what there was to experience whilst they were here? Éclair had already gone up to the dragon land in the sky with her new friends, and she was completely happy. At least, for the time being, Carlos, Maria and their companions had somewhere they could call "Home".

THE END.

Matty Millard

ABOUT THE AUTHOR

As I write this, sitting in the kitchen because my brother has had the nerve to use my spare room as an actual bedroom, Matty Millard is probably the least famous author in the world. There's a very good reason for that, and that's because this is my first book.

So far, four people have read it. They liked it though, so that's good.

I also know at least three people from Wolverhampton who would like to buy it, so as far as I'm concerned my assault on the literary world has begun.

Ever since a young age I've been writing stuff. The first thing I remember writing was a Cowboys and Indians story in a Transformers exercise book when I was about six. I'm hoping that I've improved a bit since then if I'm honest.

As a child brought up on Enid Blyton and Roald Dahl, followed by Douglas Adams and Terry Pratchett, I have a special sense of humour. I really hope that I've mixed this with my love of rock music, travelling, football and cake to come up with something that entertains you.

Printed in Great Britain
by Amazon